£14.97

LORD FOX

From *Hung-Wu and the Witch's Daughter*

Robert Nye

LORD FOX

and other Spine-Chilling Tales

Illustrated by
Sophy Williams

Orion
Children's Books

First published in Great Britain in 1997
by Orion Children's Books
a division of the Orion Publishing Group Ltd
Orion House
5 Upper St Martin's Lane
London WC2H 9EA

A catalogue record for this book is available from the British Library

Designed by Dalia Hartman

Printed in England by Clays Ltd, St Ives plc

ISBN 1 85881 234 8

Contents

Hung-wu and the Witch's Daughter   6

Lord Fox   19

The White Raven   27

The Witches Who Stole Eyes   34

The Dragon Kingdom   45

The King of the Black Art   52

Left Eye, Right Eye   58

Orpheus and Eurydice   64

The Wooden Baby   70

True Thomas   80

Some notes on the stories   87

To John Black

Hung-wu and the Witch's Daughter

In China long ago there lived an old man who had three sons whose names were Chang, Tung, and Hung-wu. Chang was tall and Tung was strong, but Hung-wu was neither tall nor strong and his father did not think a lot of him. They all lived in a yellow house in the mountains. Every day the old man went out to look for sticks to burn on their fire.

One morning he met a widow in a white dress. She was sitting on a square stone playing chess with a blackbird. The old man liked chess, so he stopped to watch. The blackbird won every time. At last it flew away. The widow looked up.

'Would you like a game?' she asked.

'I would,' said the old man.

'Then sit down,' said the widow. 'But what stakes shall we play for?'

The old man pointed to his bundle of sticks. 'We could play for that.'

The widow shook her head. 'No,' she said. 'We can't play for sticks because I don't have any sticks. What else have you got?'

'Nothing,' said the old man. 'I am poor, you see.'

'Don't you have any children?' demanded the widow.

'Well, yes,' said the old man in surprise. 'I have three sons.'

The widow clapped her skinny hands. 'Just right,' she cackled. 'I have daughters. Let us play. If you win, I will send my daughters as brides for your sons. But if I win, you must send me your sons to marry my daughters.'

The old man did not much like this idea. But he thought to himself: If she could not beat a blackbird then I am bound to win, for I am certainly a better player than any bird. So he nodded his head and sat down on the square stone.

They played three games and the widow won each game. It was dusk when

7

they finished. The widow stood up and pointed to a dark valley. 'That is where I live,' she said. 'Tomorrow you must send me your eldest son. Three days later, the second son. And three days after that day, the youngest son.' Then she gathered all the chess-men in her apron and went off.

The old man returned home. He told his sons what had happened. Chang and Tung were pleased, for they wanted to be married. But Hung-wu was scared when he heard the story, and gnawed at his pigtail.

The next day the old man sent Chang to the widow's house in the dark valley. Three days later, he sent Tung. And three days after that day, he sent Hung-wu.

Hung-wu had not got far when he met a philosopher wearing a green hat, who asked him where he was going.

'I am going to the house of the widow in the valley,' Hung-wu said.

'What for?' asked the philosopher.

'To marry her youngest daughter,' said Hung-wu. 'My two older brothers are there already. They have married her other daughters.'

The philosopher took off his hat and shook the snow from it. 'Unfortunately for you,' he said, 'that widow is a witch. She doesn't have three daughters. She lives in the valley in a big black house, and she has only one daughter. The girl is certainly beautiful, but her mother uses her to trick men to the house and when they come - she kills them! Your brothers are dead. Your eldest brother was eaten by the lion that waits by the outer door. Your second brother was eaten by the tiger that waits by the inner door.'

'Oh dear,' cried Hung-wu. 'What shall I do?'

'Well,' said the philosopher, 'you were lucky to meet me.' He took an iron pearl from his pocket. 'Throw this to the lion by the outer door,' he said. Then he took an iron rod from his boot. 'Give this to the tiger by the inner door,' he said. He pointed to a cherry tree that was growing by the stream. 'Cut a branch from that tree,' he said, 'and when you reach the third door, push the door open with it, and you will go in safely enough.'

Hung-wu took the pearl and the rod, thanked the philosopher, then went and cut a branch from the cherry tree that grew by the stream. He hurried on down into the dark valley.

Soon he came to a big black house. At the outer door was a lion. He threw the iron pearl to the lion, and the lion began to play with it. Hung-wu went on.

At the second door was a tiger. He threw the iron rod to the tiger, and the tiger began to play with it. Hung-wu went on. The third door was closed tight. He gave it a push with his cherry branch.

C R A S H !

A slab of iron weighing about a thousand pounds fell down as the door opened. The cherry branch was smashed to pulp. If Hung-wu had opened the door with his hand he would have been crushed to death.

The witch was sitting in her room sewing a shroud when she heard the iron slab fall. She smiled at the little blob of blood on her fingertip where the noise had made her prick herself. But she did not smile when Hung-wu came in. She wondered how he had escaped the lion, the tiger, and the slab of iron. However, she pretended to be pleased to see him.

'You've come just in time,' she purred. 'I have a jar of seeds that I want sown in the field before it rains.'

'What about the wedding?' said Hung-wu.

'When you come back, we will have the wedding,' the witch replied.

Hung-wu looked out of the window. The sky was full of fat black rain clouds. He took the jar of seeds and went out into the field. But when he got there he found the ground was so thick with weeds that he could not get the seeds in. 'How can I sow this field without a hoe or a plough?' he asked himself. He tried to pull up a few weeds, but being neither tall nor strong he soon grew tired, and lying down on the ground he fell asleep.

The wind rose and blew the rain clouds away. The sun shone on Hung-wu. He dreamt of weedings and weddings. When he woke it was evening and the field was full of pigs. The pigs had grubbed about and pulled up all the weeds. Hung-wu was pleased. He thanked the pigs, drove them away, and sowed the seeds. Then he went back to the witch.

'Have you finished the sowing?' she demanded.

'I have,' said Hung-wu.

The witch pulled a thread angrily from the shroud. 'Stupid boy,' she said. 'You didn't look at the sky, did you? All the clouds are gone, the moon is shining bright, no rain will fall, and the seeds won't grow. You will have to go and collect them all again, and not one must be missing.'

'What about the wedding?' said Hung-wu.

'When you come back, we will have the wedding.'

Hung-wu took the jar and went out into the field to search for the seeds. He looked hard. Soon his fingers were bleeding and his back ached with bending. But he had found only six seeds. He sat down to rest and stared at the moon. 'O moon,' he said. 'I am Hung-wu. I am neither tall nor strong, yet the witch wants me to find all the seeds she made me plant in this rough field. What shall I do?'

The moon did not answer. But when Hung-wu looked about him he saw a strange sight. Hundreds and thousands of red ants were swarming across the field. Each ant carried a seed. The ants dropped the seeds into the jar, and in no time at all it was full again and spilling with them. Hung-wu thanked the ants and went back to the witch.

'Have you got the seeds?' she demanded.

'Yes,' said Hung-wu.

'Every one?' said the witch.

'Every one,' said Hung-wu.

He showed her the jar.

The witch blinked and sniffed. 'Hmm,' she said. 'Well, it's far too late to have the wedding now. I'm going to sleep.'

She shut her eyes, and went.

Next morning the witch said, 'Listen, clever one. I am going to hide. If you can find me, we will have the wedding.'

Hung-wu rubbed his eyes with his little black pigtail. She had disappeared in a puff of blossom-scented smoke.

Hung-wu searched everywhere for the witch, but he could not find where she was hiding. He did not know what to do, so he sat down and gnawed his pigtail. Then he heard a voice saying, 'My mother has hidden in the garden. She has turned herself into a peach on the peach tree. You will recognise the peach because it is half red and half green. The green part is her back, the red part is her cheek. Bite her in the cheek and she will be a woman again.'

Hung-wu looked round. He saw at the window a girl in a gown the colour of the sea. Her eyes were like blue jade. Her cheeks reminded him of half-opened lotus flowers. He knew that she must be the witch's daughter. The girl smiled. Hung-wu blushed and ran out into the garden.

The peach tree was against the wall. Hanging on it was one peach, half-green, half-red, just as the witch's daughter had described. Hung-wu snatched it from the tree and bit the red side. The peach melted in his hand. It was gone. Standing in front of him was the witch, with a stream of blood running down her cheek.

'Little one, little one, did you try to kill me?' she screamed.

'Not at all,' said Hung-wu. 'I was hungry and you — I mean the peach you were — looked quite nice to eat. How could I know you were hiding as a fruit?' He grinned. 'What about the wedding?' he asked.

The witch glared at him, mopping her cheek. 'When my daughter is married,' she said, 'she will want a special bed to sleep in. Go to the palace of the Dragon King and fetch me a bed of white jade. When you have done that, we will have the wedding.'

Hung-wu's face went white as flour and his knees knocked together loudly when he heard this. The Dragon King lived in Oyster Palace at the bottom of the ocean. No one ever went there willingly. The sea was too deep. Also it had sharks in it. This time the witch seemed to have set him in impossible task.

However, while Hung-wu was standing scratching his head unhappily under the peach tree the witch's daughter appeared from the house. She carried a golden fork in her hand.

'I heard my mother say that you must bring her a bed of white jade from Oyster Palace, where the Dragon King lives,' she said.

Hung-wu nodded. The witch's daughter was so beautiful he could not speak when he looked at her.

'Just take this golden fork,' said the witch's daughter. 'If you draw a line on the sea with it, a road will form and you will be able to go anywhere you want.'

Hung-wu, his tongue still in a knot, smiled his thanks and took the fork. He went down to the shore. When he got there he drew a line on the water. The waves rolled back on either side of the line and there in front of him was a salty road leading straight to the palace of the Dragon King. Hung-wu marched down it, his pigtail swinging from side to side.

When he reached Oyster Palace he did not waste time. He saw the Dragon

King and told him what he wanted, and why.

'A bed of white jade?' repeated the Dragon King, downing a jellyfish cocktail in one go. 'Just look in the store room, my dear boy. There are plenty of white jade beds in there. I can't abide 'em, myself. Give me bad dreams. Choose any one you like, dear boy, and have it with my best wishes. Fancy a jellyfish?'

Hung-wu was pleased. He thanked the Dragon King, managed to avoid a jellyfish, and chose a bed. Then, carrying the bed on his head, he went back along the road which he had carved in the water with the golden fork.

When the witch saw the white jade bed her eyes bristled like buttons. 'Clever clever little one,' she purred. 'Clever clever clever little pigtail!' And she seized Hung-wu's pigtail in her skinny hands and twisted it hard, all the time smiling as though this was a friendly thing to do.

'What about the wedding?' demanded Hung-wu.

'Ah, ah, the wedding, the wedding,' chanted the witch, making out that she had forgotten about it. 'Listen, pigtail. In the west, on the mountain of the Monkey King, there is a big drum. We will need it for the celebrations. Go to the mountain of the Monkey King and fetch me that big drum. When you have done that, we will have the wedding.'

Hung-wu shivered all the way down to his toenails. He had heard that the Monkey King was fierce and wild. He lived on Desolation Mountain. Still, Hung-wu knew that he would have to go.

Just as he was leaving the house, the witch's daughter appeared again. 'What task has my mother set you now?' she asked.

Fear helped Hung-wu speak to her. 'I have to go and fetch the big drum from Desolation Mountain, the home of the Monkey King,' he explained.

The witch's daughter sat down and thought for a moment. First she rested her head on her right hand, then on her left. Then she said, 'I can tell you that the Monkey King has gone on a long journey to the Western Heaven and has not yet returned to Desolation Mountain. Now, below the mountain there is a lake of mud. Whenever the Monkey King comes home he jumps into that lake and rolls around. If you jump into it and roll around like the Monkey King, the little monkeys will think you are their master and will do anything you say. Here is a needle, a packet of lime, and a bottle of oil. Take these things with you. If you are in any danger, throw them over your shoulder – first the needle, then the lime, lastly the oil.'

Hung-wu thanked the witch's daughter for her help. When he came to the lake of mud below Desolation Mounain he held his nose between his right thumb and forefinger and jumped into it.

PLOP!

Then he rolled about in the sucky mud until his whole body was caked in it. Only his eyes showed, so that he could see where he was going. Then he hurried up the mountain.

The little monkeys swung down from the trees when they saw him coming. 'Master!' they cried. 'You've come home early!'

'Yes,' growled Hung-wu in the deepest voice he could manage. 'I came to see how you behave yourselves while I am away on monkey business.'

The little monkeys carried him up the mountain on a purple throne with poles at each end. When they reached the top they set the throne down. Hung-wu clapped his hands. 'Your master has come a long way and is very hungry,' he shouted. 'Go and get me peaches from the peach orchard and be quick about it.'

Off ran the little monkeys, squealing, to do this bidding.

When the last one was safely out of sight Hung-wu slid from the throne and ran to a silver pavilion that stood nearby. Inside the silver pavilion hung the big drum. He cut the strings that held it, balanced it on his shoulder, and set off as fast as he could down the mountainside. He had not gone far when he heard the monkeys coming after him. One of them had seen him steal the drum. 'Stop!' they shouted. 'Trickster! Thief! You pretended to be our master. Then you stole our big drum. You just wait till we catch you!'

Hung-wu took the needle from his muddy pocket. He threw it behind him. As soon as it hit the ground there was a needle mountain behind him and the angry monkeys. The monkeys tore their skin and scratched their eyes on it, but it did not stop them. They howled and screamed as they came over the needle mountain.

Hung-wu took the packet of lime the witch's daughter had given him and threw it over his shoulder. As soon as that hit the ground there was a mountain of lime between him and the monkeys. With their torn skin and blind eyes some of the monkeys got stuck in the lime and died. But the rest still chased him, angrier than ever.

Hung-wu took the bottle of oil from his pocket. He threw it behind him. The bottle burst, and the oil came pouring out. Immediately there was a slippery mountain between him and the monkeys. When the monkeys tried to climb up the slippery mountain, they slipped straight down again, and when they climbed up again, they slipped straight down again . . . So Hung-wu escaped, washed all the mud off in a stream, and returned to the witch before the sun had set.

'Surely it is time for the wedding now?' Hung-wu said to the witch, when he had given her the big drum of the Monkey King.

The witch pointed with her finger to the sun. 'It's early yet,' she whined. 'My daughter will need a net to keep the mosquitoes from her bed of white jade. Just go into the garden and cut down two bamboo sticks. When you come back, we will have the wedding.'

Hung-wu thought to himself: Two bamboo sticks? That sounds too easy to be true.

He went to the witch's daughter. He did not feel so frightened of her being beautiful now, so he told her what her mother had asked him to do and asked her what was terrible about the garden.

'What is terrible about the garden,' said the witch's daughter, 'is the gardener. His name is Nung-kua-ma and he has a body like a bull, a head like a tiger, and sharp teeth and claws. He likes to tear off people's skins and eat their fingers.'

Hung-wu bit his pigtail. His eyes rolled. 'What can I do against such a monster?' he stammered.

The witch's daughter went to a long lacquered chest and took out a coat of coconut, ten small reeds, and a two-edged hatchet. She hung the coat on Hung-wu's shoulders, fitted the bamboo reeds on his fingers, and gave him the two-edged hatchet to hold. 'Be as quick as you can,' she said, 'and you will come to no harm.'

Hung-wu thanked her and went into the garden. He found the bamboo and cut down two sticks with his hatchet. Just as that moment the gardener came out of the thicket.

'AAAAAAAAAAAAAAAAAAAAAAAAAAAAAAAAAAAAAAAAAAAA,' he roared. His claws caught Hung-wu and stripped the skin from his back – only it

"The little monkeys carried him up the mountain on a purple throne with poles at each end."

was not Hung-wu's skin that came off, only the coconut coat. Then Nung-kua-ma the terrible gardener used his sharp teeth to bite off Hung-wu's fingers – only it was not the fingers that he crunched, only the ten small reeds. He stuffed the coat and the reeds into his hairy mouth and began to eat them, stamping his feet as he did so. Hung-wu ran off.

The witch was playing dice with dead men's bones. When she saw that Hung-wu had escaped from Nung-kua-ma and brought the bamboo for the mosquito net, she said, 'Clever clever little one, clever clever clever clever little one! Oh how very clever you are, little pigtail!'

Hung-wu was wise to her tricks. He skipped out of reach when she made to twist his pigtail. 'I have sown seeds and gathered seeds,' he said. 'I have found you when you hid in the likeness of a peach. I have brought you a bed of white jade from Oyster Palace where the Dragon King lives, and a big drum for celebrations from Desolation Mountain where the Monkey King lives. Also bamboo for a mosquito net to keep your daughter comfortable at night. Surely now it is time for the wedding?'

To his surprise, the witch patted him on the head. 'Yes, dear,' she said. 'It *is* time for the wedding.' She pinched his cheek. 'But first,' she said thoughtfully, 'you really must have something to eat. You haven't eaten all day, have you, pigtail? You must be very hungry.'

'I am,' Hung-wu admitted.

'In the black pot in the kitchen you will find some noodles,' said the witch. 'Eat them first. When you come back, we will have the wedding.'

Hung-wu hurried to the kitchen. He was so hungry. He took the lid off the black pot. There were lovely white noodles inside. He grabbed a handful and stuffed them into his mouth. Soon he felt a terrible pain. He rolled on the floor and kicked his legs in agony.

The kitchen door opened. It was the witch's daughter. 'What is the matter?' she cried.

Gasping, Hung-wu told her.

'Quick!' she said. 'Take off your shoes and hang upside-down on that beam there!'

'But why –?'

'Don't argue!'

Hung-wu shook off his shoes and hung from the beam upside-down with his knees bent over it and his pigtail trailing the floor. The witch's daughter snatched a shoe in either hand and began beating him with them. Before long, a snake fell out of Hung-wu's mouth. And then another. And then another. Soon there were ten small white snakes wriggling and writhing on the floor. The witch's daughter went on beating Hung-wu with the shoes until he had coughed up all the snakes.

Then she helped him down. 'My mother always wants to harm you,' she said. 'Those were snakes you ate, not noodles. It is lucky you are not dead. Go straightaway and ask my mother to have the wedding now.'

Hung-wu thanked her, and did as she said.

The witch stamped and cursed and tore out handfuls of her own hair, but she could think of no more tasks or excuses, and she had to agree to the wedding taking place the next evening.

The wedding of Hung-wu and the witch's daughter was a magnificent affair. The big drum of the Monkey King was beaten. The bed of white jade from the palace of the Dragon King stood ready for them in a huge hall, with a mosquito net made from bamboo hanging over it. But when Hung-wu and his bride approached the bed they found a golden river flowing down the middle of it.

'This is another magic of my mother's,' said the witch's daughter.

She searched everywhere for the source of the spell. At last, in a cupboard, she found a jug of tea with a bit of wood floating in it. She took out the wood, emptied the tea on the floor, and the river vanished at once.

'We must run away,' she whispered to her husband. 'If we stay here, my mother will certainly try to kill us.'

She snatched up a blue umbrella and a chicken, gave them both to her husband to carry, and they fled away in the middle of the night.

The moon shone bright yellow on the Chinese mountains. They had not gone far when they heard a whirring sound above their heads. The witch's daughter opened the blue umbrella and beckoned Hung-wu to shelter with her beneath it.

'My mother has sent a flying knife after us,' she explained. 'If that knife smells blood, it falls. Throw out the chicken, and the knife will kill it.'

Hung-wu did as he was told. The knife flashed down. The chicken squawked. Then it was dead.

They hurried on along the mountain road. But the witch's daughter got a stitch. She had to stop for breath.

'Listen!' she cried.

Hung-wu listened. He could hear the whirring sound high in the air again.

'It's the flying knife,' hissed the witch's daughter, as they cowered beneath the blue umbrella. 'It's still after us! Chicken blood is sweet. Human blood is salty. My mother knows she did not kill us last time. What can we do?'

Hung-wu felt brave because he loved her. 'I will step out,' he said. 'I will sacrifice myself.'

'No, no,' said the witch's daughter. 'I must die, because I can come to life again. When I am dead just carry my body home with you and buy a big pail to put it in. In seven times seven days I shall come to life again.'

So saying, and before Hung-wu could stop her, she stepped out from beneath the shelter of the blue umbrella. He heard the knife zoom down. Then its noise ceased. Hung-wu saw his bride lying on the ground. Her eyes were closed. Her face was as pale as pear blossom. The knife was stuck in the heart and blood was pouring out. Hung-wu wiped away his tears with his little black pigtail and carried her body to his home.

It was dawn when he reached his father's house. He told his father all that had happened. The old man wept when he heard how Chang and Tung had been killed by the witch. But Hung-wu bought a big pail, put his bride's body in it, put the lid on, and watched and waited.

After forty-eight days, Hung-wu heard groans and moans coming from the pail, as if someone was in unbearable pain. He thought to himself: If I don't let her out now, but wait another day, she might die again.

So he took the lid off the pail.

The witch's daughter lifted up her head slowly and looked at him. 'Why did you uncover me a day too soon?' she said. 'Obviously we are not meant for each other after all.'

Tears ran down her face. Then her head sank back and her eyes closed. She was dead for ever.

Lord Fox

T here was once a young woman called Lady Mary who had two brothers called Forbes and Edward. They lived together in the wild border country between England and Scotland, in a fine house which stood on a cliff overlooking the sea. Lady Mary was beautiful, and she had more men wanting to marry her than she could count on the fingers of both hands. Forbes and Edward were very proud and very fond of their lovely sister, and anxious that she should choose well amongst her many suitors.

Now amongst these suitors was a certain Lord Fox. Lord Fox was handsome and rich and witty, though nobody seemed to know much about him. He was new to the border country, it was said.

Lady Mary was charmed by the company of this Lord Fox. Her brothers Forbes and Edward were also charmed, and Lord Fox came back again and again to the house on the cliff. It was a strange thing, as Lady Mary soon noticed, but they never needed to send him an invitation. Forbes had only to mention Lord Fox's name to Edward, or Edward had only to say something to Forbes about Lord Fox, and there he would be, strolling towards them across the lawn in sunlight peeling off his elegant black mittens or leaning in the doorway toying with the hilt of his sword, nodding and smiling and wishing them good day.

As for the Lady Mary herself, she had only to think of handsome Lord Fox, and lo, he appeared. He dined with them, hunted with them, sailed with them in the bay, and went with them for long walks on the shore looking for shells and starfish, which latter he likened to the dropped gloves of angels. The man's supply of amusing remarks was endless. He was so gallant and so gay that everyone liked him. And he wooed Lady Mary so well that before long she promised to marry him.

Then Lady Mary asked Lord Fox where they would live when they were married.

'Why, in my house, my dear,' Lord Fox replied.

'But where is this house of yours?' asked Lady Mary.

'Oh, you can't miss it,' said Lord Fox, smoothing his spiky black moustaches. 'It's called Bold House, my darling, and it's a very fine place indeed.'

Lady Mary was puzzled. 'But which direction is it in from here?' she asked him.

Lord Fox waved his white hand gracefully in the air. 'North of the north,' he said, 'east of the east, south of the south, and west of the west.'

Then he laughed.

'That sounds a long way away,' remarked Lady Mary.

'Not at all,' said Lord Fox, smiling his most extreme smile. 'In fact, you'll be surprised how near it is, my sweet.'

This conversation baffled Lady Mary. She was even more baffled when at other times Lord Fox talked a great deal about this very fine house of his where he would take her when they were married, without once offering to show it to her, or inviting Forbes and Edward to come and see it either.

'When we are married,' Lord Fox told her. 'That will be soon enough.'

Now the Lady Mary was a lass of spirit, and these answers did not satisfy her at all. So one day, just before the wedding, she made up her mind to go and see Bold House if she could. She put on her best embroidered gown of grass-green silk, and set out alone to look for it.

Really, the Lady Mary did not know what to expect. It seemed impossible to find a house that was north of the north, east of the east, south of the south, and west of the west. But the mystery was a challenge to her, so she tried.

As it happened, she found Bold House in no time at all. In fact, it was quite near, just as Lord Fox had said it was. Lady Mary could not understand how she had never noticed it before. It was a big house, with high walls and a deep moat, and it had a big black door.

Lady Mary went up to that door and knocked. There was no answer. Lady Mary knocked again. The doorknocker was cold in her hand. There was still no answer. As she stood there, Lady Mary noticed that over the portal of the door were carved the words:

BE BOLD, BE BOLD

So Lady Mary knocked a third time. And this time the big black door swung slowly open.

There was nobody there on the other side of the door. Lady Mary thought to herself that the door could not have been properly locked, which meant that perhaps Lord Fox was at home but had not heard her knocking. So she went in.

The hall of Bold House was long, and as cold as a tomb. Lady Mary passed down it. The walls were hung with tapestries that seemed to writhe as she went by them. At the end of the hall she came to a broad spiral staircase.

'Lord Fox?' called Lady Mary. 'It's me, your bride to be. I've come to visit you.'

There was no answer. The house seemed quite unoccupied. So Lady Mary went slowly up the stairs.

At the top of the stairs she came to a great gallery. It had been cold downstairs, but up here in the gallery it was freezing. The walls glistened with frost. The gallery itself was roofed with black ice, like the inside of a wolf's mouth. Lady Mary drew her shawl about her, shivering.

Above the entrance to the gallery were carved the words:

BE BOLD, BE BOLD, BUT NOT TOO BOLD

The Lady Mary crossed herself. Then she took a deep breath and went on down the gallery. Her grass-green gown made a swishing sound as she went. Otherwise the house was as still and as silent as a tomb.

At the end of the gallery, Lady Mary came to another black door. This door was small and narrow. Over the portal of the narrow black door were carved the words:

BE BOLD, BE BOLD, BUT NOT TOO BOLD,
LEST THAT YOUR HEART'S BLOOD
SHOULD RUN COLD.

Now the Lady Mary crossed herself again, as a shiver ran down her spine. But she was a lass of spirit, and having come this far she was not going to turn back through any fear. With a trembling hand, she turned the key in the tight lock. She opened the door.

The room beyond the door was lit with candles. By the light of these flickering candles, the Lady Mary saw that all round it, some hanging by their necks from hooks in the rafters, some seated on chairs, some lying on the floor, were the bodies and skeletons of dozens of beautiful young women in their wedding-dresses that were all stained with blood. The floor was thick with coils of human hair.

Lady Mary did not scream. She shut the door. She went to the window for air – and saw Lord Fox!

He was coming towards the house across rank lawns. It had begun to snow and his figure, dressed all in black, loomed like a devil in a mist of whirling white flakes. He snowed towards the Lady Mary. He was whirling. He carried a thin sword in his left hand. With his right hand he dragged a young girl by the hair. The girl was screaming. But Lord Fox said nothing.

The Lady Mary sprang back from the window. She snatched up her grass-green skirts and ran through the gallery. She hurried down the spiral stairs. But then she heard the front door opening. Lord Fox was coming! There was nothing for it, Lady Mary knew, but to hide herself as quickly and as best she could. So she hid behind a big wine-butt that stood in a corner of the hall, just at the foot of the staircase.

Lord Fox entered the hall, dragging his victim behind him. As for Lady Mary, crouched behind the wine-butt, her heart was beating so loud that she thought he would hear it.

But Lord Fox did not hear her or see her, he was so bent on his own cruel business.

He began to drag the poor girl up the stairs.

The girl did not go easy. She screamed. She kicked. Begging for mercy, she caught hold of a knob at the turn of the banisters. Lady Mary, peeping up from her hiding place, saw the girl's hand tighten. There was a diamond ring on one of her fingers. As Lady Mary watched, helpless, Lord Fox raised up his sword and cut off the girl's hand. The poor girl fainted. Hand and diamond ring fell into Lady Mary's lap where she crouched behind the wine-butt!

Lady Mary heard Lord Fox going down the gallery, and the dragging sound of

*"He carried a thin sword in his left hand. With his right hand he dragged
a young girl by the hair."*

the girl behind him. As soon as she heard the door to the Bloody Chamber kicked open, the Lady Mary jumped up and ran. She ran, ran, ran from Bold House, she ran through the snow, and she did not stop running until she reached the safety of her own house on the cliff.

Now it happened that the very next day the marriage contract of Lady Mary and Lord Fox was to be signed, and there was a splendid wedding breakfast before that.

Lady Mary sat at table in her bridal gown, with Forbes on her right hand and Edward on her left. And there was Lord Fox, sitting opposite her, looking so gay and so gallant.

Lord Fox was busy making his usual witty remarks, but Lady Mary sat stroking spoons on the tablecloth and saying nothing. At last, when she would not laugh or even smile at any of his jokes, Lord Fox turned to her and said:

'How pale you are this morning, my dear.'

Lady Mary kept her eyes downcast on her lap.

'Yes,' she said. 'I had a bad night's rest last night. I had horrible dreams.'

Then Lord Fox smiled and said, 'Dreams go by contraries, my darling. But tell me your dream, and your sweet voice will serve to speed the time till I can call you mine.'

'I dreamed,' said Lady Mary, 'that I went yesterday to seek that house which is to be my home when we are married. And I found it in the woods, with high walls and a deep moat, and above its great black door the words, BE BOLD, BE BOLD, were written.'

Lord Fox stopped smiling. He sat frowning at Lady Mary. Then he spoke in a hurry. 'But it is not so, nor it was not so,' said Lord Fox.

Lady Mary did not look at him. 'In my dream,' she said, 'that door opened for me, and I went into your house, and I passed down the hall, and I went up the stairs, and I came to a gallery, and above the entrance to that gallery the words, BE BOLD, BE BOLD, BUT NOT TOO BOLD were written.'

Now, Lord Fox was frowning so hard at Lady Mary that he looked as if he was trying to think her out of existence. 'But it is not so, nor it was not so,' he muttered.

'Then I dreamed,' said Lady Mary, 'that I went on down the gallery, and at the end of the gallery I came to another black door, a narrow black door, and above that door more words were written, and this time the words said:

> BE BOLD, BE BOLD, BUT NOT TOO BOLD,
> LEST THAT YOUR HEART'S BLOOD
> SHOULD RUN COLD.'

'It is not so, nor it was not so!' cried Lord Fox. He was sweating now. His eyes went to and fro.

'And then, in my dream, I opened the door,' said Lady Mary. 'I opened the door, and the room beyond was filled with the bodies and skeletons of poor dead women, all stained with their own blood.'

Lord Fox said nothing. He sat as still as a stone. But they could hear his teeth grinding.

'In my dream then,' said Lady Mary, 'I saw you from a window, and you were dragging a young girl by the hair, Lord Fox. And I dreamed that I ran downstairs, and that I just had time to hide myself behind a wine-butt before you came into the house with your victim. In my dream, Lord Fox, you dragged that poor girl up the stairs, and she clutched at a knob in the turn of the stair-rail, and you out with your sword, Lord Fox, and you cut off her hand.'

Then Lord Fox rose in his seat and glared about him wildly as if to escape, and his eyeteeth showed like those of a fox beset by dogs, and his face was as fierce as the core of a naked flame.

And he whispered, and his voice was like dead leaves rustling on the ground:

'It is not so, nor it was not so. And God forbid it should be so!'

Then the Lady Mary rose slowly in her seat also, and she looked straight at Lord Fox, her eyes blazing, and her voice rang like a bell as she cried:

'But it is so, and it was so! *Here's hand and ring I have to show!*'

And with these words she pulled out from her bosom the poor lifeless hand with its glittering diamond ring, and pointed it straight at Lord Fox.

The devil squealed and roared with rage. He ran to the door. But Forbes and Edward had locked it, for they had known, known from the start, that their sister's dream was not a dream at all.

Then Lord Fox was at the window, clawing, foaming at the mouth, trying to jump out of it. But Forbes and Edward were too fast for him. They fell upon Lord Fox, and stuck him with their swords, and cut him into a thousand tiny pieces.

And the two strong brothers of the beautiful Lady Mary gathered up those thousand pieces and cast them into the sea, where they boiled and hissed and turned the water black as pitch before they sank from sight and nothing was ever seen again of that evil Lord Fox.

The White Raven

There was once a prince who lived in a dark palace in a far-away country. His poor people hated him because he was so cruel.

One day this prince was walking in his palace garden. He allowed no flowers there. On the trees no apples or oranges grew. In the heart of the garden was a deep pool of slimy green water, where no fish swam. It was always cold in the garden. Even the sunlight there seemed scared and full of ghosts.

This morning the prince was in a good mood. He had ridden out before breakfast on his horse, Satan, and burned seven cottages to cinders. Now he stood brooding in shadow. He was looking forward to the daily executions.

Just then a white raven flew down and perched on a branch of the tree under which the prince was standing.

Hatred came into the prince's eyes when he saw the white raven. He hated all birds, except hawks and vultures. He picked up a stone and threw it at the white raven. A shiver ran down his spine when the stone, in mid-air, turned into a red nose and fell to the ground harmlessly, spilling a few petals.

The white raven looked straight at the prince. It threw back its head. Its bright beak fell open. 'Amen,' it cried. 'Amen, Amen, Amen.'

The prince drew his sword and cut circles with the blade over his head.

The white raven did not move on the bough above. 'Amen,' it cried. Its voice was shrill but sweet.

Now the prince had been worried by the stone turning into a rose, so he pretended that he did not care when he saw that it seemed he could not harm the bird. He leaned on his sword, and roared with false laughter.

The white raven stared down at him for a while. Then the bird flapped its wings three times as if to shake off the shadows of the garden, and flew away.

For a week or so the prince dreamed of the white raven and what it had cried, but nothing happened to remind him of it and eventually he forgot. He grew richer and more powerful, murdering and marauding. He kidnapped the daughter of one of his lords and forced her to marry him. The unfortunate woman died giving birth to a son.

The prince hated the child. He gave it to one of the palace guards. 'Leave it in the woods,' he commanded. But the guard was not as bad as his master. He took pity on the boy. Besides, he had no children of his own and this was a grief to his wife. So instead of leaving the baby in the woods to starve or be eaten by wolves, he hid it secretly in his own quarters.

Now the prince took it into his head to have a feast to celebrate getting rid of the child. He sent out messengers with invitations. Some who were called refused to come. A few brave spirits confessed that they did not care to join in the prince's celebration of the murder of his own son. Others made less honest excuses, but still did not attend. As it fell out, only his wicked lords – the ones who were nearly as bad as the prince himself – came to the feast.

On the night of the feast they were all gathered in the great hall of the palace. The floors were paved with human bones. The walls and rafters were draped with black banners. The torches all burned blue. Every kind of meat and every kind of drink was served, and no vessel was brought to the table, brimming with drink or heavy with meat, which was not fashioned of silver. The prince himself drank wildly from a blue buffalo horn, rimmed with gold.

Now the prince had called two minstrels to the feast. One of these was all that a minstrel should *not* be: hard, bent, and ambitious. He amused the vile company with his stories and songs in praise of the devil and all his works. They banged their fists on the tables, laughing sottishly, shouting for more.

The other minstrel was different. He was disgusted by the feast, and his heart grew sad at the thought that soon it would be his turn to play. He slipped out of the hall and wandered through the passages of the palace, looking for gentler faces. But everyone was at the feast.

Passing a door in the guards' quarters, however, the minstrel heard a child crying. He pushed the door gently, then he pushed it with all his might – but it would not open. Opening closed doors was nothing to a true minstrel. He stooped down and whispered into the keyhole: 'Open lock, at my third knock!' Then he tapped three times lightly with his knuckles on the door and at the third knock it flew open and in he went.

The child was a lusty bawler. It was, of course, the prince's son. 'There's a noise,' murmured the minstrel, and sitting down by the cradle he began to rock it with one hand while plucking a lullaby from his harp with the other.

Being a true minstrel, the man was inspired to sing a song he could not understand. It was a strange song, but he knew that the song was true. He sang of a prince who was dead but not dead, lost but not lost, and who would one day come into his own and rule over the lands his father had wasted.

The child listened, and stopping its crying. Then the minstrel amused it by letting it play with his fine white gloves. The child loved this game. Before long it fell asleep clutching one glove in its fist, pressed under its cheek.

Just then the minstrel heard banging and shouting from the great hall. He took up his harp and tiptoed to the door, closing it softly behind him. He did not have the heart to take his glove away from the child who was now fast asleep.

Back in the hall the minstrel began playing and singing. His fingers gathered music between the strings, his green slipper tapped on the bone-paved floor, his voice was strong and warm.

But the prince and his guests were not pleased with the new man's songs. He sang of things they did not want to hear of.

'Long live death! Long live death!' shouted the prince, pounding on the table with his buffalo horn.

Then they all started laughing and swearing and pelting the minstrel with the bones which they had picked clean.

The minstrel took no notice. He seemed to have forgotten where he was. The bones did not harm him, either. An inch from his face they were turned, in mid-air, into roses, some red, some white. The roses fell at his feet, shedding perfume which was itself like music.

None of the guests appeared to see this. The prince, though, he saw the thrown bones turn to roses. He sat bolt-upright in his great black chair and stared at the minstrel's face. He seemed to have lost all power of speech or movement.

The minstrel played on. He played so fast and so sweet that his fingers bled.

"An inch from his face they were turned, in mid-air, into roses, some red, some white."

He sang a strange song, but he knew that the song was true. He sang of a prince who was dead but not dead, lost but not lost, and who would one day come into his own and rule over the lands his father had wasted.

And all the while the petals rose higher and higher on every side of him and his swaying harp, and he sang as though in a dream.

And then his fingers fell away from the strings, and as the last note of the strange song died among the red rose-petals and the white rose-petals and the long black banners hanging overhead, there came a roar of thunder like a hungry beast at the door, and lightning lit the blood-red windows, and a cold wind rushed through the hall, extinguishing every torch and candle.

And a white raven rode into the hall on the back of the wind and perched on the minstrel's harp.

All in the hall except the minstrel were blinded by the darkness and deafened by the wind, and they blundered about in confusion, but could find no doors.

The prince himself was not granted the mercy of being blinded or deafened. He sat still in his high-backed chair, and his eyes in the blackness shone green.

The white raven spoke.

'Amen,' it said softly. 'Amen, Amen, Amen.'

And it flew from the harp to the door.

The minstrel sat folded over his harp, his arms wrapped about it, exhausted by music. He paid no heed to the bird.

The white raven flew back and perched again on the harp.

Once more it spoke in the minstrel's ear.

'Amen,' it said, in a louder voice. 'Amen, Amen, Amen.'

Again the bird flew from the harp to the door. Still the minstrel did not move.

A third time the white raven flew back to the harp and perched on it.

This time when its beak fell open it cried with the voice of the wind and the storm, and thunder and lightning filled its throat and eyes, and it shook as though it would burst in two.

'*Amen!*' it cried. '*Amen! Amen! Amen!*'

Then the minstrel sprang up, as if awakened from deep sleep. He shook his head and he took up his harp and put it on his back. He walked softly through the rose-petals.

The white raven flew in front of him.

The minstrel followed the white raven.

'Long live death,' croaked the prince. His eyes looked pleased and clever in the gloom. But he could not rise from his chair when he tried to do so.

As for the guests, they rushed about in panic, hacking at each other with their swords, but they could find no way out.

The minstrel followed the white raven.

It flew always a little in front of him, so that no matter how fast he ran he could not catch it.

The white raven led the minstrel safely from the palace.

Outside was blackness. There was no moon. There were no stars in their usual places.

But the minstrel trusted the bird, and it led him unscathed through thicket and mire and up the mountain.

Once the minstrel stopped, because he was tired, but the white raven flew round him, clapping its wings together and crying its cry, *Amen, Amen, Amen*, so urgently that he did not dare to stop again.

Then, as bird and man reached the top of the mountain, there came out of the dark behind them a crack of thunder. The earth shook. There was a roaring and thrashing of waters. Mixed with the thunder and the sound of water, the minstrel heard cries for mercy. And, louder than all the rest, one voice that shouted defiance.

'Long live death! Long live death!'

But all soon stopped, and silence fell.

The moon came out.

The minstrel looked in wonder at the white raven. The bird returned his gaze, its eyes bright in the moonlight. Then, flying towards him, it touched him gently on the cheek with its wing, and disappeared into the night.

Now the minstrel began to feel foolish. 'What am I doing here?' he asked himself. 'I'd better get back to the palace. They'll need me for the dancing even if they don't like my songs.'

Then he wondered how he could be certain that the guests at the feast had not liked his songs. He racked his brain for memory of the night. But he could find none, until –

'My glove!' he cried. And then: 'The child!'

Certain that something dreadful had befallen the palace, and the one innocent soul in it, the minstrel started to stumble back down the mountain.

But he had not gone twenty steps when he tripped in his harp and fell flat on his face in a murmuring mountain stream.

The minstrel was wearied by the night's adventures – some of which were coming back to his mind now, in dribs and drabs of memory beyond belief. He drank deeply of the cold stream water. Then he fell asleep.

When he woke, it was morning. The sun was rising over the mountain.

The minstrel turned his head and looked down in the direction of the palace, and he saw that there was no palace. There was only water –water –water –a vast smooth silent lake stretching from one side of the valley to the other. What he had taken for a mountain stream was the nearer shore of this lake.

Shielding his eyes against the light of the sun shimmering across the lake, the minstrel saw something bobbing on the surface. It was a something now wafted towards him by the breeze, then drifting away again in the mist.

The minstrel knew what he must do.

He sat down by the lakeside and began to play his harp. He played a song calling home whenever it was that rode there on the water. The music sped ripples across the lake, and the ripples drew the theme of the harp's song back to the strings of the harp.

Presently it came to rest on the shore at the minstrel's feet. It was a cradle, and in the cradle was the child, still fast asleep, still with the white glove clutched to his cheek.

Then the minstrel took the child and looked after him all the days of his childhood as if he had been his own son. And when the boy grew up he had a new palace built on the shore of the lake, and all was grace and light inside that palace, and the minstrel, an old man now, played there at many a feast, where the hungry were filled with good things but the rich were sent empty away.

And sometimes, after the feast, the minstrel would sing quietly, just to himself and his harp.

He sang a strange song, but he knew that the song was true.

He sang of a prince who had been dead but not dead, lost but not lost, and who had come through flood and fury following one who followed a white raven.

The Witches
Who Stole Eyes

There was once a boy called Tom Fortune whose mother and father died, leaving him all alone and having to seek his own way in the world. He was a brave boy, not afraid of anyone or anything, so after he had cried for his poor mother and cried for his poor father he did not cry for himself. Instead, he set out with a red pack on his back and green leather boots on his feet, marching up hill and down dale looking for someone who would hire him. His head was high and his eyes were bright and he sang a song as he marched. This is how the song went:

> I'm Tom, Tom, Tom!
> I'm Tom, Tom, Tom!
> Tom's not afraid
> Of ANY—ONE!
>
> I'm Tom, not Tim!
> Tom! Tom! Not·Tim!
> Tom's not afraid
> Of ANY—THING!'

It was a fine song and he sang it in a loud proud voice and it certainly cheered him up although the rhymes were not very good. In this way he marched for miles until he came to a country he did not know.

The first thing Tom Fortune saw in the country he did not know was a little squat cottage that stood on the edge of a deep dark forest. In the doorway of the cottage sat an old man. He was bent and thin, with no teeth and empty black holes where his eyes should have been. He had a long beard like a ragged sleeve.

Tom could hear goats bleating in the tumbledown shed beside the cottage, and as he stood watching, flapping his red pack up and down on his back, the old man suddenly gazed up blindly at the sun, twisting his beard in his hands, and called out:

'Sorry, goats, sorry! I wish I could take you to pasture. But I can't, because I can't see, and I've no one to send with you.'

Tom chafed his green boots. 'Send me!' he cried. 'I'll take your goats to pasture, Uncle. And I'll do all the work for you as well.'

'Who's that?' demanded the old man, shivering with fright.

'My name is Tom Fortune,' said Tom, and he stepped forward and told the old man his story.

When Tom had finished he noticed that the old man had been so nervous during the telling that he had tied his beard in knots. He wondered what the old man was frightened of. However, he said nothing, but helped the old man undo the knots.

'Thank you, Tom,' said the old man, when they had done. He thought for a minute or two, rubbing his hands together as though he was washing them. Then he took a deep shuddery breath and said:

'All right, my boy, you can work for me, and welcome. The first thing you have to do is drive my goats to pasture.'

'That's easy, Uncle,' said Tom. He cut a white stick from the willow tree, to drive the goats with. Then he skipped about busily in his green boots, letting the noisy creatures out of their shed.

The old man started twisting his beard again. 'Not so fast, not so fast, Tom Fortune!' he called in his trembly voice. 'Before you go off I want to warn you about something.'

Tom puffed out his chest. 'I'm not scared of anything or anyone,' he boasted.

'Maybe you *should* be scared of some things,' said the old man. He nodded to himself once or twice, as though he had said something important. Then he said, 'Listen, whatever you do, don't let the goats go into the green glade in the forest.'

'Why not?' said Tom.

'Because,' said the old man, 'there are three witches who live there, and if you let the goats go into the green glade the witches will come and send you to sleep and then they will steal your eyes as they stole mine.'

Tom tossed his head proudly. 'I don't believe in witches,' he scoffed.

The old man said nothing. He just pointed with his stick-like fingers to the places where his eyes should have been.

A shiver made Tom's spine tingle. 'Well,' he promised, 'I'll be careful, uncle. Don't worry, I shan't let anyone steal my eyes.'

Then he drove the goats out of the yard and into the safe and sunny meadows that lay below the deep dark forest, singing his song as he went:

> *I'm Tom, Tom, Tom!*
> *I'm Tom, Tom, Tom!*
> *Tom's not afraid*
> *Of ANY–ONE!*
>
> *I'm Tom, not Tim!*
> *Tom! Tom! Not Tim!*
> *Tom's not afraid*
> *Of ANY–THING!*

Soon the goats were munching the long grass and dandelions were hanging out of their mouths.

The next day, and the day after that, Tom Fortune took the goats out to the meadows. But the day after the day after that was a very hot day, the sun glaring like a big red eye in the bright blue sky and the ground all cracked and dusty underfoot, and Tom thought to himself:

'How cool it looks in the glade over there in the forest . . . And the pasture is better besides – long, lush green grass, and daisies, and dandelions. The poor goats would love it!'

He had not forgotten the old man's warning, but he was almost ashamed to be remembering it. 'Why should I be afraid of witches,' he thought, 'when I don't even believe that there are such things?' He strutted up and down in his green boots, kicking at the ground, trying to make his mind up what to do. At last he was decided. He cut himself three long bramble shoots for luck, stuck them in his cap, and drove the goats straight into the forest, through the cool shadows under the trees, into the rich green glade. The nanny-goats ran bleating with pleasure when they saw and smelt the good grass, and the billy-goats put down their heads and butted each other to get at the best bits, but soon they all settled down to crop and munch contentedly. Tom Fortune sat down on a stone in the shade.

He had not been sitting there long when he looked round and saw that a girl was standing beside him. Tom rubbed his eyes. He had not seen her come walking through the trees. It was as if she had appeared out of sunlight. The girl was dressed in white linen from head to foot, but her hair was as black and glossy as a raven's wing and she had eyes like blackberries glistening with dew.

'Good morning, Greenboots,' she said.

'Good morning,' said Tom, looking somewhere else.

She was the most beautiful girl he had ever seen.

The girl smiled. 'My name is Beauty,' she said.

'Hello Beauty. My name is Tom,' said Tom.

'Hello Tim,' said Beauty.

Tom frowned. 'Not Tim,' he said. 'Tom.'

'Are you sure?' demanded Beauty.

'Of course I'm sure,' said Tom. 'T.O.M. Tom. That's me.'

'Well, you don't look much like a Tom and that's certain,' said Beauty. 'If ever I saw a Tim – it's you! T.I.M. Tim. Short for *timid*, I daresay.'

Tom went red in the face and was just going to say something angry when Beauty took an apple from her sleeve and went on quickly. 'I expect you didn't know that over there, deep in the forest, there's an apple tree, and that the apples that grow on the tree are the sweetest apples in all the world. And I'll tell you why you didn't know. Because you're scared to go into the forest, aren't you, Tim? And even if you did go, you'd be scared to eat one of the apples!'

Tom stamped his foot. 'My name is TOM!' he shouted. 'And I'm not afraid of anything!'

Beauty smiled sweetly and held out the apple to him. 'Go on then,' she murmured. 'Eat it.'

Tom took the apple in his hand. He longed to sink his teeth into it, and prove Beauty wrong, but something made him stop. He noticed that although the apple *looked* good it did not shine in the sun as you would expect a red apple to shine. Also, it felt soft and heavy in his grasp.

Tom rubbed the apple suspiciously against his cheek. It had no smell at all. 'Did you pick it just for me?' he asked.

'Yes' said Beauty.

'Why?' said Tom.

Beauty smiled again. 'Because you have such lovely blue eyes,' she said.

Tom blinked. So that was it! There *were* such things as witches. This girl was a witch – and she was after his eyes. If he ate the apple he would surely fall asleep as the old man had warned, and then Beauty would steal his eyes.

He shook his head. 'No thanks,' he said, 'I don't want the apple. My master has an apple tree in his garden all dripping with apples better than yours. I've eaten my fill.' And drawing back his arm he threw the poisoned apple as far into the forest as he could.

Beauty was angry, but she still made her face smile. 'Very well,' she purred. 'Now I *know* that your name is Tim!'

And she walked off into the forest, singing a bitter little song.

About an hour passed. Tom Fortune sat dreaming in the shade, watching the goats champ and munch. He saw a buzzard high in the blue sky overhead, like a full-stop scratched in the sun. Then he noticed that another girl was standing at his elbow. She was more beautiful than the first girl. She had golden hair and was dressed in green. In her right hand she held a white rose.

'Good morning, Greenboots,' she said.

'Good morning,' said Tom.

The girl smiled. 'My name is Truth,' she said.

'Hello Truth. My name is Tom,' said Tom.

'Hello Tim,' said Truth.

Tom took a deep breath. 'Not Tim,' he said. 'Tom.'

'No,' said Truth. 'I don't think so. If you were a real Tom you wouldn't be frightened of me. And you are frightened, aren't you?'

'Not in the least,' said Tom, although he was.

The girl held up the white rose. 'In that case,' she murmured, 'I suppose

"Then he tied them up with the brambles."

you won't be afraid to smell how sweet this rose is. I picked it in the forest just for you.'

Oh yes, thought Tom, and if I do smell your rose I will fall asleep and you will steal my eyes!

So he shook his head, and said, 'No thank you, Truth. My master has even sweeter roses in his garden. I have smelled all the roses I want.'

Truth's face went dark with rage when Tom refused the rose. She threw the flower to the ground and crushed it with her heel. 'Please yourself, *Tim*,' she muttered, and stalked off into the forest without another word.

Noon came and went. Tom Fortune watched the goats and played with the brambles he had stuck in his cap. It was very hot and he would dearly have liked to stretch out in the shade and enjoy a nap, but he did not dare do this in case the witches came and stole his eyes. He was not surprised when a third girl appeared at his side. She was the youngest and most beautiful of them all. She had long red hair and was dressed in a dark gown.

'Good afternoon, Greenboots,' she said.

'Good afternoon,' said Tom.

This girl did not smile. Her eyes and lips were sad. 'My name is Innocence,' she said.

'Hello Innocence. My name is Tom,' said Tom.

'Hello Tom,' said Innocence.

Tom Fortune was so pleased that she had called him by his right name that he forgot to be suspicious when Innocence took a silver comb from her dark sleeve, saying, 'What a handsome boy you are, Tom Greenboots. But your hair is all sticky and untidy with the heat. Lie back and let me comb it for you!'

Innocence came closer, her lips still sad, the silver comb in her outstretched hand. 'Oh Tom,' she murmured, 'such pretty blue eyes you have! Such pretty little sweet little lovely little nice blue eyes!'

Tom jumped to his feet before she could plunge the silver comb into his hair. Snatching up his cap he took one of the bramble shoots from it and smacked at Innocence's hand.

The witch – for, of course, she *was* a witch gave a high-pitched scream. Because Tom had dared to strike her all her powers were gone. She began to cry, for she could not move from the spot.

'Beauty!' she shrieked. 'Beauty! Truth! Sister witches! Help! Help me!' Her voice was like that of a hare caught fast in a trap.

Tom Fortune hardened his heart to her crying, remembering that she would have picked out his eyes if he had given her half a chance. Quickly he twined the bramble round and round her wrists.

Beauty and Truth came running out of the dark forest. When they saw what Tom had done to their sister they began to beg him to unbind her and set her free, promising him anything if he would.

'Unbind her yourselves!' said Tom.

'We can't!' cried Beauty.

'Our skin is softer than mortal skin,' explained Truth. 'The bramble would prick and tear us!'

All the same, when they saw that Tom was determined to keep their sister prisoner they went to her aid, trying to unpick the bramble that bound her. As soon as they did that, Tom sprang upon them and struck them both on the hands with the other bramble shoots. Then he tied them up with the brambles.

'You wicked horrible Greenboots!' wailed Beauty.

'You cruel unfeeling mortal!' howled Truth.

'Just wait till we're free!' screamed Innocence. 'We'll scratch out your eyes, you miserable boy!'

Tom shook his head. 'How dare you say I'm horrible to stop your tricks?' he demanded. 'Witches who steal eyes deserve all they get!'

And, so saying, he ran home helter-skelter through the forest to tell his master the news.

'Uncle!' he cried. 'Come with me!' And he grabbed the old man by the arm.

'Where are we going?' asked the old man in confusion.

'You'll see!' promised Tom. 'Yes,' he added, 'you'll see all right, because *we're going to get back your eyes!*'

Tom Fortune led his master to the green glade where he had left the three witches. They were still there, weeping and wailing and trying to break their bramble bonds.

Tom went up to Beauty. 'Now,' he said, 'You tell me where my master's eyes are and I'll set you free. But if you don't tell me . . . then I'll throw you in that stream over there!'

Beauty shook with fright. 'I don't know where his eyes are,' she said sulkily.

'Right,' said Tom, his face grim. 'Into the stream you go!'

Now witches are like cats only more so. The thought of being pitched into running water filled Beauty's heart with terror. She knew that she must drown.

'Don't throw me in, Greenboots,' she begged. 'Please, please, dear kind generous Greenboots, don't throw me in the water! I'll give you your master's eyes!'

Tom undid her bonds and followed warily as the witch led him to a cave in the forest.

The cave was full of eyes! There were big eyes and little eyes, bright eyes and weary eyes, blue eyes, brown eyes, hazel eyes and amber eyes, hawk eyes and bat eyes, eyes as sharp as needles and eyes oozing tears, all sorts and shapes and sizes and colour and condition of eyes.

Beauty picked up a pair of eyes from the pile, and gave them to Tom. Tom ran back to the old man, dragging the witch behind him. Then he set the eyes in his master's head.

'Can you see, Uncle? Can you see?' he cried excitedly, skipping round and round him.

'Yes!' shouted the old man. 'I can see! But all I can see is mice and shrews and voles and moonlight! Too-whoo! Too-whit!' And he stretched out his scraggy arms and rocked to and fro on his heels making hooting noises.

The witches laughed wickedly. Tom Fortune grew very angry.

'These are not my master's eyes!' he cried. 'You gave me owl's eyes!' And he seized Beauty by her long black hair and threw her into the water, where she drowned.

'Now,' Tom said to Truth. 'You fetch my master's eyes this minute or it will be the worse for you!'

The witch began to make excuses and say she did not know where they were, but when Tom Fortune seized her by her golden hair and dragged her through the forest to the cave where the eyes were heaped she went in to the pile and chose another pair and brought them back to him. Tom ran to the old man and set the new eyes in his head.

'Can you see, Uncle? Can you see?'

'Yes!' cried the old man. 'But, oh dear, oh dear, all I can see is snow and wastes and woods and sledges and – *Ooooow! OOOOOOW! I would* like a fresh young lamb to eat!'

'Wolf's eyes!' said Tom grimly. And he caught Truth and threw her into the water, where she drowned too.

'Now,' Tom said to Innocence. 'You tell me where my master's eyes are! And no tricks, or it's in the stream you go to join your sisters!'

At this, the witch began to wring her hands and moan, saying she did not know where the old man's eyes were – but Tom Fortune would take no nonsense. He dragged her to the cave and told her to fetch them quickly. Innocence went in to the pile and chose another pair and gave them to him without a word.

Tom ran back to the old man and set the new eyes in his head.

'Can you see, Uncle? Can you see?'

'Yes!' cried the old man. 'But all I can see is reeds and water and pebbles and old boots and lots of little fishes I want to gobble up!'

'Pike's eyes!' said Tom.

He was so furious at having been deceived three times that he seized Innocence by her long red hair and dragged her to the water's edge.

'Spare me!' she pleaded. 'Spare me, Tom Greenboots, and I promise that this time I will bring you your master's own eyes without fail!'

Tom took pity on her. He remembered that, after all, she was the only one who had called him by his proper name. Hand in hand they went back together through the forest to the cave and Innocence went in to the pile and drew out a pair of eyes that were right at the bottom, underneath all the others.

'These are your master's eyes,' she said, giving them to Tom.

So Tom ran back to the old man and set the eyes in his head. This time the old man clapped his hands for joy.

'I can see!' he cried, dancing round and round on his spindly bent legs. 'Yes, these are my eyes . . . A slight squint in the left, perfect vision in the right! Oh, it's good to have them back! Hurrah! I can see again at last!'

Tom turned to the witch Innocence.

'Thank you,' he said.

'That's all right, Tom Greenboots,' said Innocence. 'I'm only sorry that they were ever stolen. I'm only sorry that I was ever a witch to do such things. I'll never do it again!'

Then Tom Fortune and his master went back together through the forest to their little cottage, where they lived happily ever after. Every day Tom took the goats out to pasture and brought them home and milked them. The old man made the milk into cheese, and they both ate the cheese.

The Dragon Kingdom

Urashima Taro was a fisherman. He lived long ago, in the province of Tanba, in the south-west of Japan. He was not married. His father was dead, and he lived with his mother. She was always nagging him to take a wife and leave home, but Urashima used to say:

'I can't afford it. Wait till I catch more fish.'

He never did catch many fish because he was rather a lazy man. He liked to sit and watch his nets drift in the clear blue water, with their cork floats bobbing up and down – but he didn't really care for catching fish.

One winter the wind blew from the north for three long weeks, and it was impossible even to launch the raft to go out fishing. There was not much to eat, and Urashima grew quite worried.

At last, one night, the north wind dropped and the sky began to clear. There was a big yellow moon and a lot of stars. Urashima went down to the harbour and sailed out to sea on his raft.

He fished in the moonlight all night but he did not catch a single fish.

Dawn came. Still no fish.

Urashima was very hungry and worried.

He fished on.

The sun rose high in the sky.

Not a sign of a fish, until in the early afternoon there was suddenly a lovely ripple across the surface of the sea, like the strings of a harp being plucked, and then, all at once, Urashima felt something underwater tugging his big net away.

'A sea bream!' he shouted, and pulled the net in.

It was not a sea bream.

It was a turtle.

Now, turtles were no use. They scared the fish away. So Urashima threw the turtle back into the sea, far away from the raft, and went on fishing.

About the middle of the afternoon, Urashima felt his big net fill again.

He hauled it in.

No fish. Just the same turtle. It had a brown shell that sparkled in the sun and big blue eyes like pieces of sea. However, Urashima was in no mood to admire it.

'Go away!' he cried.

The turtle just looked at him. Its eyes were very deep and wise.

'Back to the bottom of the sea!' cried Urashima.

The turtle did not budge.

Grunting, Urashima picked up the turtle and held it high over his head. Then he threw it as far as he could. The turtle sank with a mighty splash.

'Turtles are useless,' said Urashima to himself. 'Turtles are just bad luck,' he added, casting his net out again.

By now he was so hungry that he had a pain. Trying to forget it, he lit his pipe and sat smoking as he went on fishing. He dangled his feet in the warm water and watched the sun sink down in the west.

As the sun touched the sea another slow and lovely ripple passed across the surface, and Urashima felt his net shiver and fill again. He dragged it in quickly, thinking that this time surely he had caught a good fat sea bream . . .

But it was the same turtle.

Urashima stared at it.

The turtle looked back at him.

'Will you please leave me alone?' said Urashima.

The turtle blinked. Its blue eyes were cloudy with tears.

'I'm going home,' said Urashima. 'And I shall hope never to see you again.'

So saying, he pushed the turtle away from the raft. It swam in a slow circle around him – once, twice, three times. Then it sank below the darkening waves and out of sight.

Urashima was tired and dispirited and very very hungry. The moon came up like a great yellow cheese and he wished he could take a bite out of it. He sat for a while smoking and sighing and thinking about all the fish that he hadn't

"There was a palace made of corals and sea crystals, with white sharks on guard duty."

caught. Then he decided that he had better start to go home. He wondered what he would say to his mother.

Urashima was paddling the raft along in the moonlight when he noticed a strange ship in the distance. It was a sailing ship, with a tall mast and a wide black sail. The strange thing about this ship was that although it was coming through the water towards him at a great speed its sail was not puffed out in the way you would expect, with the wind filling it. Instead, the sail was quite a hollow shape, as though the wind was blowing *against* it.

Urashima was frightened.

He steered his raft to starboard, but the black ship still came at him.

He steered his raft to port, but there was no escape – the black ship still came at him.

Now it was right alongside the raft, and Urashima saw that the captain was a skeleton.

'Urashima!' cried the captain.

'Yes?' said Urashima, his knees knocking together.

'Come on board my ship,' said the captain.

'Not likely,' said Urashima.

'Don't be silly,' said the captain. 'We have come especially for you from the Princess of Ryugu.'

'Never heard of Ryugu,' said Urashima.

'Well,' said the captain, 'it's the dragon kingdom at the bottom of the sea.'

'Well,' said Urashima, 'if I went to the dragon kingdom my mother would be left all alone, so I can't go, thanks very much all the same.'

The skeleton captain laughed. It was an extraordinary sound – like bones dancing, or a lot of plates falling downstairs. 'We will see that your mother is taken care of,' he promised. 'Now, little fisherman, come aboard. As a matter of fact, you have no choice.'

This was true. Urashima found that his feet had some kind of spell upon them and they walked him forward even though he didn't want to go.

As soon as he was on board the black ship, it sank!

Down, down, down it went.

Down and down to the world at the bottom of the sea.

It was a wonderful place when you got there, the dragon kingdom of Ryugu.

There was a palace made of corals and sea crystals, with white sharks on guard duty. Just as Urashima was rubbing his eyes and getting used to being so many fathoms undersea, a gong sounded and the Princess of Ryugu appeared at his side.

'I expect you must be hungry,' she said. 'What would you like for dinner?'

'Do you have any dried rice and pickled plums?' asked Urashima.

'We have all kinds of good Japanese food,' said the Princess with a smile. 'Make yourself at home.'

'Talking of home,' said Urashima, 'I'll have to be getting back to my mother.'

The Princess nodded. Her blue eyes were very beautiful and friendly. 'Don't worry,' she said. 'Just stay two or three days and enjoy yourself here with us under the sea. Then you can go home to your mother and tell her all your adventures.'

The dried rice and pickled plums were delicious. Urashima was well content. The Princess gave him new shoes and a new kimono too. There was nothing to do except sit about eating, or sifting sand like gold-dust through your fingers, or watching all the silver fish at their endless ballet.

In this way, days, then weeks, then months passed, without Urashima really noticing. The Princess was very kind to him and he liked her a lot. As a matter of fact, she reminded him of someone, but he could not remember who. She had smooth brown skin and eyes the same colour as the sea of her kingdom.

At last, when Urashima thought that about three years had passed, he decided that it really was time he went home. When he told the Princess what he was thinking, and asked her permission to leave, she said:

'Of course. No one ever stays here against their will.'

Then she went to a great sea chest and took a little ivory jewel-box out of it.

'This is my gift to you,' she said. 'It has three compartments. Don't open it until you need to.'

Urashima took the box and thanked her. Then he went back on board the black ship with the skeleton for captain, and the ship sailed up, up, up, until it reached the southwest coast of Japan.

Urashima left the ship and went to his village and looked around.

It was all changed.

Where he remembered trees, there were now no trees.

He could not understand it.

The houses were all different too, and he did not recognise any of the people.

'How could this have happened in just three years?' he thought to himself. 'I know – I must go and ask my mother.'

So he made his way to his own house, but when he got there he found that his own house was changed too. It was a different colour and there was thatch on the roof where before there had just been slates.

Urashima looked in at the window.

His mother was not there.

Instead, he saw an old man weaving silk in a corner.

Urashima entered the house, and greeted the old man. They talked about silkworms for a while, and then at last Urashima said:

'Tell me, do you know a man by the name of Urashima Taro?'

The old man laughed. 'I don't believe in that,' he said.

'What do you mean?' asked Urashima.

'It's a story for children,' said the old man. 'They tell them that long long ago, about the time when my grandfather's father was just a boy, there was this fisherman called Urashima who went to the dragon kingdom at the bottom of the sea. He never came back.'

'And what became of that man's mother?' asked Urashima.

'She died, of course,' said the old man. 'Just remember – if it was true, that would have been more than a hundred years ago. But we know that it's not true, don't we?'

Urashima said nothing.

He went into the garden. Yes, there was the little cherry tree he had planted for his mother. But it was old and dry and withered, with no blossoms on it.

Urashima's eyes filled with tears. What was he to do. He had come home and no one knew him. Then he remembered the little ivory jewel-box and the Princess saying, 'Don't open it until you need to.' He took it from the pocket of his kimono, and looked at it. Was *now* the right moment? Would he find his way back to the dragon kingdom?

Urashima opened the first compartment. In it was a white crane's feather.

Urashima opened the next compartment. A puff of white smoke came from it, and his hand holding the box was suddenly old.

Urashima opened the last compartment. In it there was a mirror. He looked in the mirror and saw to his amazement that he had become an old old man.

Then a very magical thing happened.

First, the old cherry tree burst into bloom.

Then, a slow and lovely ripple spread right across the evening sky.

Then a sweet voice said:

'Back to the bottom of the sea?'

Urashima looked round. He could see no one.

The voice said:

'Sick of the sight of me?'

Urashima rubbed his eyes. There was no one there.

But the voice said:

'Do you really hope never to see me again?'

And as the voice said this, the white crane's feather from the first compartment flew up in the air and attached itself to Urashima's back.

Now he could fly!

Urashima Taro flew over the house, over the village, over the harbour and down to the shore. He had turned into a white crane. And there on the shore, waiting for him, was a turtle with eyes the same colour as the sea of her kingdom.

And the crane and the turtle danced together, and they are dancing still.

The King
of the Black Art

❦

There was once an old fisherman and one day when he was out fishing he caught a long box in his net, and inside the box when he opened it was a baby boy.

The fisherman took the baby boy home to his wife, and they brought him up as their own child.

When the boy reached his fourteenth birthday he was walking on the harbour wall when he saw a fine ship riding in the bay, and on the bridge of the ship there was a man dressed all in gold who was juggling three silver balls with spikes on them.

'Do you see these silver balls?' the stranger called out across the water.

'I do,' shouted the boy.

'They have poison in them,' the stranger cried.

Now the boy was impressed that this man would dare to juggle three silver poison-balls with spikes on them. When the ship came to land the stranger came on shore, and he seemed to take a great fancy to the boy. He offered to take him away for a year and a day, and to teach the boy his art. He wheedled so well that the old fisherman and his wife agreed, and the boy sailed away with the stranger.

In a year and a day the ship came back, and the boy was back, strutting on the fine deck of the ship, juggling seven silver poison-balls with spikes on them. The old couple were so pleased that they allowed the stranger to take the boy for another year and a day, so that he might teach the boy more of his art.

But this time the boy did not come back.

So the old wife sent the fisherman to look for him. The fisherman sailed far across the sea until he came to a land where he had never been, and then he travelled on and on in the strange land until he came to a forest and in a hut in the middle of the forest he met an old man who asked him in for the night.

The fisherman told the old man his story, and the old man said, 'There's little doubt that it is the King of the Black Art who has your son.'

'The King of the Black Art!' cried the fisherman in dismay. 'What can I do?'

'I don't know,' admitted the old man. 'But my brother might be able to help you. He lives a week's march from here. Tell him I sent you.'

So the next morning the fisherman set out, and he journeyed for another week until he found another hut even deeper in the forest, and in this hut there was another old man. If the first man had been old, this old man was three times older. But he asked the fisherman in, and gave him food and lodging, and told him what to do.

The fisherman, said the old old man, was to go on until he reached the King of the Black Art's castle, and then when he got there he was to ring the great bell that hung outside it and ask for his son. They would laugh at him, warned the old old man, and the King of the Black Art would tell him to choose his son from among fourteen pigeons that he would toss up into the air, and he was to choose a little, weak, raggety-winged one, that flew lower than the rest.

The fisherman did as he was told.

He came to the King of the Black Art's castle, he rang the great bell that hung outside it, and he asked for his son. When the King of the Black Art laughed at him and told him to choose his son from among fourteen pigeons that he tossed up in the air, the fisherman chose the raggety-winged pigeon that flew lower than the rest.

The King of the Black Art was angry.

'Take him, and be damned to you both!' he roared. In a trice the boy was standing there beside the fisherman and they went away together from the castle.

'I'd never have got free if you hadn't come for me,' the boy said, as they walked along. 'The King of the Black Art and his two sons are at the head of all the wizards in the world. But I've learned a trick or two while I've been in their company, and we'll get something back from them if you do as I tell you.'

The fisherman was frightened, but he agreed.

'Right,' said the boy. 'Now, we're coming to a town where there is a market. Before we get there I will change myself into a greyhound. All the lords and gentry will offer to buy me, but don't you go selling me to anyone until the King of Black Art comes. You can take five hundred pounds from him, but mind you, father, for your life, do not sell the collar and strap off the greyhound's neck. Take off that collar and strap and put it in your pocket before you give him the greyhound.'

The fisherman and the boy came to the market. The boy turned himself into the finest greyhound dog that ever was seen. Knights and nobles came crowding round the fisherman bidding to buy the creature, but he would take no offers until he saw the King of the Black Art and his two sons hurrying into the place, and then he would not let them have the dog until they gave him five hundred pounds for it.

Then the fisherman took the strap from round the dog's neck, and tied a piece of string round it instead, and walked away with the strap in his pocket.

As soon as he was out of town, the fisherman removed the strap from his pocket, and there was his son standing beside him, for he had been the strap.

They went on to another town, and the son turned himself into a grand stallion horse, but he warned his father not to sell the bridle with the horse, whatever he did. The knights and nobles came round him as before, for no such horse had ever been in those parts; but the fisherman would not sell the horse to anyone till the King of the Black Art and his two sons came hurrying up, and then he demanded a thousand pounds for him.

'He looks worth that,' said the King of the Black Art, 'and I'll give it if he is as good as his looks. But no man can buy a horse without riding it.'

The fisherman stood his ground for a while, but the King produced a great bag of gold pieces worth much more than a thousand pounds, saying, 'Just let me ride him round the fairground once. You can hold this bag of gold pieces while I do it.'

The glint of the gold was too much for the fisherman.

'Very well,' he said.

Then the King of the Black Art leapt on the horse's back and rode away on him, bridle and all.

The fisherman turned with tears in his eyes to look at the gold, but it turned

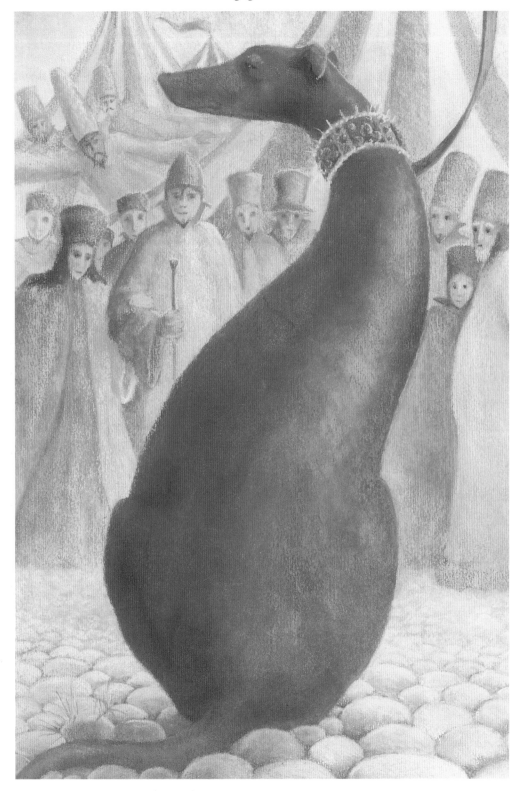

"The boy turned himself into the finest greyhound dog that ever was seen."

to dung in his gaze, and when he looked back, the horse and its rider were gone.

The King of the Black Art rode the stallion to a stable where he was fastened up and given not a drop to drink. Before long, the stallion's tongue was all swollen and coated.

One day the King of the Black Art and his two sons went out hunting, and as a groom walked past the stall where the stallion stood with his tongue hanging out a voice said:

'Give me a drink, I beg you!'

The groom was very frightened to hear a horse speak. Of course, it was not the horse speaking, but the boy in the horse's bridle. He went on begging and begging, until the groom had compassion on the horse, and led it out to the stream.

'Just loosen the bit so that I can drink,' said the boy.

The groom loosened the bit. As soon as he did this, the boy changed out of the bridle and slipped into the stream as a salmon. But as he did so all the bells began to ring in the castle of the King of the Black Art, and the magicians dashed back from the hills.

Realising what had happened, the King of the Black Art and his two sons turned themselves swiftly into otters, and swam after the salmon. They came closer and closer, until they were almost on him, but at the last minute he leapt high out of the water and turned into a swallow in the air.

The swallow darted off, but the otters turned as quickly into hawks, and went after him.

The swallow saw a lady sitting in a garden, flew down to her, and turned into a ring on her finger.

The hawks came. They swept round the lady and then flew away.

Then the ring spoke.

It said: 'Lady, in a few minutes three labourers will come into this garden, and offer to build up your dyke. When they have done it, they will ask you for the ring from your finger in payment. But when they do that say to them that you would rather throw it into the bonfire, and throw the ring as you speak.'

The lady promised that she would do as the ring told her, and in a few minutes the three labourers arrived. They built up the walls as if by magic, and when the lady offered them money, they asked her for the ring, but she threw it into the bonfire.

Then the labourers turned themselves into three blacksmiths, and began to blow up the fire in search of the ring, but the ring hopped out on the other side of the flames and went into a pile of corn and quickly turned itself into a grain in the pile.

The magicians turned themselves into three cocks, and began to gobble the corn, but the boy turned into a fox, and snapped off the heads of the three cocks as quick as thought.

So the King of the Black Art was at last defeated, and the boy rejoined his father, and they lived happily and prosperously all their days by means of his magic art.

Left Eye,
Right Eye

An old midwife and her husband once went to Caernarfon to hire a servant-maid at the All-Hallows Fair. The custom in those days for the young men and women who wished to be hired, was for them to stand at a certain spot. When the old couple reached it they at once noticed a girl with hair as red as fire, standing a little apart from the others. The midwife went up to her and asked if she wanted a job. 'If it pleases you, madam,' said the girl politely. She told them that her name was Eilian and that she was nineteen. A few days later she came to take up her new appointment.

At that time – all this took place, as you might guess, many years ago in Wales – it was customary for the womenfolk to do the spinning after supper during the long winter months. The first night she did the spinning Eilian began to weep.

'Why, what's the matter, child?' asked the old woman.

'It's the light,' complained Eilian. 'It's the lamp hurting my eyes.'

'I suppose next you'll be asking us to buy a new one especially for you?' snapped the old man sarcastically, for there was nothing he hated more than a lot of talking while he smoked his evening pipe.

'Oh no, sir,' said Eilian, 'I'm sure such a thought never crossed my mind.' She ran to the window and peered out through the frost-ferns, then she turned back to the puzzled couple, her cheeks glowing. 'The moon is shining so rich and bright! Now if I might just take my spinning-wheel down to the meadow, I'm sure I could work very well.'

Her mistress looked at her sharply. 'Are you mad, girl? Spinning outdoors, at this time of night!'

Eilian said nothing, but spread out her hands imploringly.

'Let her go,' muttered the old man, puffing at his pipe and reaching for a piece of coal with the tongs. 'If she doesn't catch her death of cold she might even do a spot of spinning to keep warm. Heaven knows she'll never do any in here, moaning about a perfectly good light and what else.'

Eilian tossed back her red hair, smiled, curtsied, took up her spinning-wheel, and skipped out of the cottage.

The clock ticked, the cat purred on the old man's lap, the old woman got on with her darning. After a while she looked up and said, 'Do you think I ought to go and see if she's all right? It's cold enough to turn a body to ice out there.'

'Leave her be,' advised her husband. 'It's only some flighty notion. She'll be back in a minute and only too pleased with the old lamp, you watch.'

But Eilian did not come back, and when the hands of the clock both pointed to twelve the old man, who had fallen asleep in his comfortable chair, was suddenly awakened by his wife shaking him and whispering excitedly, 'Sssh! Come quick! You won't believe your eyes when you see what I've just seen!'

Grumbling, half of him still in a dream about a vegetable marrow as big as the Houses of Parliament, the old man allowed her to push him to the window. Looking out, he came wide-awake in a moment. 'My whiskers!' he cried. 'It's the Fair Family!'

And so it was – the Fair Family, or little people, or, as some call them, the Lordly Ones who dwell in the hollow hills. They were dancing and singing in the frosty, moonlit meadow. And in the middle of the green and golden company sat Eilian, the servant-maid, her spinning-wheel turning so fast that sparks seemed to fly from it and stars get caught in it, her red hair tumbled about her shoulders, her face glowing with delight.

The couple dared not tell the girl what they had seen, but they treated her with great respect and care from that time on. Every night when there was a fair white moon she would take her spinning-wheel down into the meadow, and on these occasions an enormous amount of work was done. She never seemed to feel the cold and even went out in crisp deep snow to spin among the Fair Family. The midwife and her husband were well pleased, if a little frightened, to have such an industrious maid-servant.

One spring evening, however, just about sheep-shearing time, Eilian went out as usual with her wheel to the meadow, but did not come back. She did not come back the next night, nor the next. The old couple found her wheel, with her work piled neatly beside it, but they were sad to have lost Eilian. 'She has gone with the Lordly Ones,' said the old woman, and her husband, sucking thoughtfully at his pipe, agreed that this was probably what had happened.

Some months after Eilian's disappearance, on a night of fitful moonlight and drizzle falling through thin mist, there came a clatter of horse's hooves outside the cottage and then a fist banged on the door.

The old man opened it, the poker concealed in his right hand behind his leg, for the hour was late and they were not expecting any visitors.

A stranger stood on the step, his face in the shadows.

'Sir,' he said, 'I believe your good lady is a midwife. Would you kindly ask her to come with me? It's for my wife. Please be quick.'

The midwife put on her cape and bonnet and got up behind the stranger on his horse. He rode away wildly through the moonlight, as fast as a swallow, up hill and down dale, through bramble and bush and briar, covering miles of darkness before the old woman had time even to cry, 'Oh!' At last he drew rein before a deep cave. Dismounting, the stranger took the old woman's arm. He led her into the cave and then through a door at the far end of it and into a chamber where his wife lay in bed. It was quite the finest place the old woman had ever seen in her life: thick carpets on the floor, tapestries on the walls, and the bed like a galleon of the night, with silken pillowcases and velvet curtains and blankets made of ermine.

In an hour the midwife's work was done, and the lady had been delivered of a bonny baby boy. As the old woman was dressing it in its tiny nightgown and shawl before the fire in the enormous log-filled grate, the stranger came up to her with a bottle of blue ointment in his hand.

'Would you please rub a little of this on the child's eyes?' he said. 'But take care that you do not touch your own eyes with it, or I'll not be responsible for the consequences.'

The old woman did as she was asked, being careful not to let any of the blue ointment go near her own eyes. But, as she was putting the bottle away, her left eye began to itch and without thinking she put the finger to it that she had used for anointing the baby's eyes. Immediately, the whole scene was changed – but only to that eye, for the curious thing was that the midwife now found two rooms before her. With her right eye she saw everything as fine and luxurious as it had seemed to be, but with her left eye she saw a damp, dripping, uncomfortable cave, with a miserable fire flickering in one corner, and the poor mother lying not in a richly-brocaded bed but huddled on a bundle of rushes and withered ferns, with stones all around her. And she saw that the woman was none other than her former maid-servant, Eilian.

She said nothing, not even when with her left eye she noticed little men and women dressed in green and gold hurrying in and out with dainty food for Eilian, their every movement as light as the morning breeze; but when morning came, and she was packing her bag ready to depart, she leant close over the bed and whispered, 'You've many friends now, eh, Eilian?'

The girl started, and stared at her. 'Yes, I have,' she replied. 'But how do you know? And how do you know me?'

Then the old woman explained that she had accidentally applied some of the baby's blue ointment to her left eye.

'Well, just you take care that my husband doesn't find out what you've done,' advised Eilian. And she told the midwife her story. How she had been helped with her spinning by the Fair Family, on condition that she married one of them. 'I thought I could outwit them,' she said, with a wry smile, 'and never really intended to fulfil my part of the bargain. I always used to take a twig of rowan with me into the meadow, for no Lordly One dare cross or touch the rowan, and I thought that way they could never carry me off. But the day we helped shear Bower's sheep I was so exhausted I forgot to take the twig with me. And here I am!'

'But you're happy, aren't you, Eilian?' the midwife asked.

'Indeed I am,' said Eilian, kissing her baby. 'But it's what you see with your left eye that is the real world I live in now, and though it's hard enough it's no grief to me. The right eye is all illusion.'

Some time after, the old woman – who had been taken home by the stranger, on horseback, just as she had come, and given a purseful of gold for her services – happened to be late in getting to market.

"Immediately, the whole scene was changed — but only to that eye."

'I reckon the Fair Family must be here today,' joked the greengrocer. 'I've had six apples stolen already, and hark at the noise!'

And the Fair Family *were* there. The old woman could see them with her left eye, swarming about amongst the stalls. Noticing Eilian's husband standing close by and nodding to her, she stepped up to him and said, 'Fine morning. And how is Eilian?'

'Oh, she's very well,' replied the Lordly One.

'And the baby?'

'Coming along fine,' said the Lordly One. 'But tell me – with what eye can you see me?'

'With this one,' said the old woman, pointing.

Then the Lordly One snatched up a bulrush and pulled out her left eye before she could move or shout. And from that day forth the old woman's right eye had to do the work of two, and she saw only the world that Eilian had told her was illusion.

Orpheus and Eurydice

O nce upon a time, in Greece, and long ago, there was Orpheus.
Orpheus was a marvellous musician. When he was just a boy he
had learned how to play the lyre – an instrument with strings, quite
like a harp. He practised until he was very good. In fact, Orpheus was not just
very good. He was the *best*. No one ever made music as lovely as the music that
came from his lyre – no one before, and no one after. Orpheus was the finest
musician who ever lived.

When he played, spiders stopped their spinning, ants stopped their scuttling
in the ant castles, bees forgot to gather in the pollen for their honey, and
even the little songbirds stopped singing and listened and tried to catch the
tune. Everything stopped and listened when Orpheus played. His music was
magic.

As he grew older, his music grew more magical. He used to go and sit on a
rock outside his village, and there he would play all day long. There was a
snake that lived under the rock, but even the snake was enchanted by the
sweet sounds that came from Orpheus's lyre. It used to coil itself up, and sway
to and fro in time to the music. All the creatures of the forest came to listen to
Orpheus, too. There were lions and tigers and wolves and bears, foxes and
owls and eagles and hawks, wild pigs, little rabbits, cats, and lizards, and mice.
You might think that the cats would catch the mice, or that the mice would be
worried by the cats, but they weren't, because of the music.

Because of the music all those different creatures were at peace with one
another, and happy.

Even some of the trees of the forest came to listen. They pulled themselves up by their roots, and came and stood in a circle around Orpheus, so that they could hear better.

Orpheus was glad to have trees in his audience, because Greece is a hot country and making music all day is hard work. The branches of the trees made a pleasant shade where he was playing.

When Orpheus grew up and was a man, he married Eurydice. They were very happy together. When they wanted a house, Orpheus just played a few notes on his lyre and great stones and boulders came rolling along to listen. Orpheus played a house-building song and the stones rolled themselves on top of each other until there was a place to live.

Every day Orpheus used to go to the rock outside his village, and sit there, and play upon the lyre. And every day Eurydice used to go too, and listen to his music.

One morning, though, Eurydice went for a walk on her own in the meadows. As she went, she danced. And as she danced, she remembered one of her husband's best tunes, and hummed it to herself.

When she reached the rock where Orpheus usually sat and played all day, Eurydice stopped to pick a flower. As she picked the flower she accidentally trod on the snake that lived under the rock. That snake was always gentle and harmless when it was under the spell of Orpheus's music, but now there was no music and it was a killer. It turned, instantly, and bit Eurydice in the ankle, and she fell down dead.

In those days, when people died they went to a place called Tartarus. Tartarus was the Underworld. The King of Tartarus was called Pluto, and its Queen was called Persephone. Pluto and Persephone made Eurydice welcome and were kind to her, but of course she did not like being dead and in the Underworld. She would rather have been alive and back in her home with Orpheus.

Orpheus went looking for Eurydice. He could not find her anywhere. She had disappeared completely. He took his lyre, and he played all his best tunes, singing and calling his wife's name all the time.

'Eurydice! Eurydice!'

The hills rang with the name, and the mountains echoed it, but there was no answer.

Now Orpheus realised that Eurydice must be in the Underworld. He could not bear the thought of her being dead, so he made up his mind that he would go down there and play his music for King Pluto. He thought that perhaps he would be able to persuade Pluto and Persephone to let Eurydice come out of Tartarus and back into the world again.

Orpheus took his lyre and went down through deep dark caves into Pluto's kingdom.

Once he was there, in Tartarus, he started playing.

Oh, how he played!

His music had been brilliant before. But now it was not just brilliant, it was full of feeling. Before, it had come from Orpheus's head. Now, it came straight from his heart.

He played and he played, until his fingers were quite scarred from plucking at the strings of the lyre. And the song that he played was so sweet and so sad that it brought tears to the eyes of all who heard it. Even Pluto, that hard-hearted King, could not help weeping at the music.

When the song was over, Orpheus said:

'Give me back my Eurydice!'

'On one condition,' said King Pluto.

'Anything!' cried Orpheus. 'I love her so much!'

Pluto wiped the tears from his eyes. 'I heard that in your music,' he said, 'and that is why I am letting your wife go back with you out of Tartarus, and into the world again. But there is one other thing which a man should have, as well as love, and that thing is faith. You must have faith that Eurydice is following you as you go up and out of Tartarus, and you must not once look back to see if she is really behind you. If you turn to look back, before she reaches the place where the dark of the Underworld gives way to the light of the sun, then she will be lost to you for ever.'

'But if I don't look back?' said Orpheus. 'If I have faith, and don't look back?'

'Then she will be safe,' King Pluto said. 'And you will both live for ever.'

So Orpheus started back again, back up the long dark winding track that leads out of the Underworld, away from Pluto's Kingdom. And as he went, he played upon his lyre.

The music was not sad any more.

"So Orpheus started back up again...And as he went, he played upon his lyre."

It was full of life and hope and dancing. It sounded like a carnival.

Orpheus was so happy to be getting his beloved Eurydice back.

But now a curious thing began to happen. The more Orpheus played his happy music, the more he wondered if it could be true. Before, he had just played without thinking, and the tunes had come, and he had never once stopped to wonder about them, or to question them. But now he felt that so much depended upon his music.

Was Eurydice really behind him?

Or was King Pluto tricking him?

The light began to grow at the end of the tunnel. Orpheus quickened his stride. He rushed on. He stumbled. But he kept on playing. His fingers went blindly across the strings of the lyre, and all the while, at every stride now, his own happy music seemed to mock him:

Is Eurydice really behind me?

Or is King Pluto tricking me?

Orpheus had almost reached the tunnel's end. He could feel the breeze that blew down into the caves of the Underworld. He could see the sunlight glimmering in the cave mouth. He was nearly there . . .

A cunning thought came into his head. If he played quietly, he might be able to hear Eurydice's footsteps behind him. His hand slowed on the strings of the lyre. The music hushed to a whisper. He strained his ears for any sound from behind him . . .

Not one! Not a sound! All at once, as he stepped out of the tunnel and into the sunlight, Orpheus was sure that Pluto had tricked him. He *turned round*. . .

There was Eurydice, right behind him!

But even as he watched her arms stretch out towards him, Orpheus realised that he had lost her for ever.

She was fading. She was streaming backwards into the Underworld. She was becoming a ghost.

Orpheus had broken the condition. He had looked back. He had not had enough faith to get his wife safely out of Tartarus. Eurydice was lost!

Orpheus knew that he could not go again into Pluto's Kingdom. A man may journey once into the Underworld, and strike a bargain with its King, but never more than once.

Orpheus felt that he could not go back to his home either, to the village where he had been a boy, to the valley where he had sat upon the rock and played his lyre to all the animals and trees. Instead, he wandered for the rest of his life, grieving for Eurydice, playing such terribly sad songs upon his lyre that the songs broke the hearts of all who heard them.

No one really knows what happened to Orpheus in the end. Some say that he was struck by lightning. Some say that he was torn to pieces by the Maenads, wild women who wander in the mountains.

All that is certain is that the music stopped. No one ever heard it anywhere.

But they say that his lyre was seen again, the magic lyre of Orpheus, and that it came floating down the river Hebrus from the mountains, and then out to sea, where it was tossed here and there by the waves until one day it was cast up on the shore at the island of Lesbos. It lay there in the sand, until it was all overgrown with flowers, and half-buried under falling leaves.

And they say that the nightingales sing more sweetly on that island than in any other place in the world.

The Wooden Baby

Krog was a woodcutter. He lived with his wife Mog in a green cottage on the edge of a black forest. They were very poor. Every morning Krog went off to work with his bright axe over his shoulder. He wore big boots and trousers made of moleskin. Mog stayed at home and spun flax. She wore a bonnet and sang hymns as she turned the spindle. When Krog came back every evening at sunset they sat down to dinner. All they had to eat was turnips. They had turnip soup, turnip chops, and turnip jelly. It was horrible and they were very thin.

One night Mog put down her wooden spoon and said: 'I wish we had a baby.'

'A baby?' said Krog. 'We couldn't afford it. We haven't enough to eat ourselves. How could we feed a baby?'

Mog sighed. 'I suppose you're right,' she said. 'All the same, I'd like one.'

The next night she said the same thing. And the next night. And the one after that. Krog was a patient man, so he did not complain or get angry. But when Mog started talking about babies in the morning too, he grew sick of the subject. There were not enough turnips to have breakfast – dinner was their only meal – and he hated making commonsensical remarks on an empty stomach.

One morning, after a whole week of listening to his wife talking about babies, Krog was out as usual chopping wood in the forest when he saw a tree that looked like an old man. It was black and bent, with long twisting roots that poked up through the cracked earth like dirty toenails. This gave him an idea. He stopped and stared at the tree, wiping the sweat from his face. Then he turned back to his log, cut it neatly in half, stripped off the bark and began slicing and chopping at the white wood. He shaped the end until it was round and smooth like a baby's head. He gave it a body, and arms, and legs. He trimmed the roots to make them look like fingers and toes. When he had finished it looked just like a real baby.

Krog took it tenderly under his arm and ran home. Mog was sitting in the porch with her bonnet on, spinning flax and singing hymns. Krog held the wooden baby behind his back so that she would have a surprise.

'Heavens,' said Mog, 'what are you doing home so early? You'll lose your job!'

'Never mind that,' said Krog. 'Look what I've got!'

And he held it up for her to see.

His wife was so amazed she had to take her bonnet off to let the air to her head. 'A baby!' she cried.

'A wooden baby,' said Krog. 'Well, do you want it?'

Mog clapped her hands. 'Yes, yes, of course I do,' she said. She took the baby from him, hurried indoors, and wrapped it in the tablecloth. Krog went back to the forest to work, pleased that she was pleased. When he reached the place where he had left his axe he noticed that the tree like an old man seemed to be shaking its head at him in the wind. But he ignored it.

Meanwhile, Mog was sitting in the parlour, rocking the baby in her arms and singing a song to it:

> *Lullaby, hushaby,*
> *Little wooden baby boy.*
> *When you wake, my pet, my sweet,*
> *You shall have some food to eat.*
> *Lullaby, hushaby.*

All at once the wooden baby started to wriggle about in the tablecloth. It kicked its legs. It turned its shiny head. Then it began to scream and shout.

'Food!' it bellowed. 'Food! Food! Food! I want food to eat!'

Its voice was so loud that the words cracked every piece of crockery on the dresser. The cups crashed to the tiled floor, leaving only their handles swinging on the hooks.

Mog did not know whether to laugh or cry. 'Oh dear,' she said. 'I didn't mean it. I thought that you wouldn't really want anything, being made of wood, that is. I can't —'

'FOOD!' roared the wooden baby. And this time its shout shattered the windowpane and made the kettle explode.

'Sshh, sshh,' soothed Mog. 'I'll get you something, my poppet. Just wait a minute. It won't take a moment. I'll make you some nice turnip porridge, how's that?'

The baby glared at her. Its face was very red and it had eyes like knots. It did not look as though it much fancied the idea of turnip porridge. But it lay quietly enough while Mog lit the fire and stirred the pot.

When the porridge was ready, Mog wiped her hands on her apron, took her own spoon from the drawer and began feeding the baby. The fat lips gobbled greedily. The throat gurgled as the porridge slid down. When it was all gone the baby belched.

'Pardon!' said Mog.

The baby looked at her. It took a deep breath.

'Food!' it shouted. 'Food! Food! Food! I want food to eat!'

'Goodness,' said Mog, 'the poor thing *is* hungry. Never mind, my jewel. I'll get you something as quick as I can.'

There were no turnips left, except those for Krog's supper. So Mog rushed out of the house with a pail in her hand, ran down the road, found a cow in a field, milked it, and hurried back. The baby did not give her time to pour the milk into a jug. As soon as it saw her coming it reached out one greedy hand and grabbed the pail. It drank all the milk in one gluttonous gulp, creamy suds running down its chin. Then it gave a terrible belch that made the house shake and dust fly out of the cushions.

'Pardon?' said Mog, doubtfully.

The baby looked at her. It rolled its eyes. It took a deep breath . . .

'No!' cried Mog. 'Don't shout! Please, please don't shout again. I'll get you something. I will. I promise. Only —'

'FOOD!' roared the baby. 'FOOD! FOOD! FOOD! I WANT FOOD TO EAT!'

The shouts were so loud they made the chimney fall off. A crow that had been nesting there was so frightened that all its feathers dropped out. It flapped away into the forest, bald and squawking like a chicken.

Now Mog was a proud woman, and although she had always been poor she had never borrowed in her life. But she had to do something to quench the wooden baby's enormous appetite. So she ran down the road to her nearest neighbour and begged for a loaf of bread. When she got back the baby was asleep. It lay on its back, snoring. The noise was like thunder. Mog crept in and put the loaf on the table. Then she went out into the yard to draw water from the well to set on the fire for soup.

All the flowers in the garden were trembling in time with the baby's snores. Suddenly they stopped. Mog looked nervously at the house. The baby had woken up.

'FOO – !'

The ear-shattering shout broke off before the word was finished. The baby had evidently seen the loaf. Mog smiled to herself.

'Such a sweet little thing really,' she murmured.

But when she went back into the parlour to make breadcrumbs for the soup she found that the loaf was gone. The 'sweet little thing' had not just *seen* it. It had eaten it! The whole loaf! And, what was worse, the baby was growing fatter and fatter and hungrier and hungrier with every tick of the clock. Before Mog's eyes, it started eating the tablecloth, stuffing it into its mouth and chewing, chewing, chewing. Its eyes rolled. Its cheeks bulged. With a huge gulp it swallowed the lot.

'Mercy on us!' cried Mog. 'Will you never stop?'

The baby looked at her. It was now as big as a barrel. It opened its mouth to shout.

'Hush!' Mog pleaded. 'Don't ask for more! You've eaten all I have!'

The baby blinked. It peeped through its chubby wooden fingers at her. This time it did not shout. But its quiet voice was more dreadful than its loud voice. 'That's right,' it said. 'I've eaten all you have – and now I'm going to eat you too!'

And it did. Before Mog could move the baby jumped on her and gobbled her up. In a minute all that was left of her was her clogs, her bonnet, and her hymn-book, lying on the floor beside the big fat wooden baby.

Krog came home early from the forest. As he unlatched the little green gate he heard a terrible bellow from the kitchen.

"'What do you think you're laughing at?' howled the baby, stepping into
the garden on its wobbly legs."

'Food! Food! Food! Food! Food! *I want food to eat!*'

Krog dropped his axe and ran into the parlour. The baby was trying to eat the carpet. He hardly recognised it — it had grown so fat.

'Help!' cried Krog. He looked round for his wife. 'Where's your mummy? Mog! Mog! Where are you, Mog?'

The baby stood up. Its tiny legs could scarcely support it. Its belly was like a small mountain.

'No use shouting for mummykins,' it said softly. 'I've eaten her.'

'You've *what*?' said Krog.

'Eaten her,' said the baby. 'And now I'm going to eat you too!'

And it did. Before Krog could move the baby jumped on him and gobbled him up. All that was left of him was his big boots and his moleskin trousers.

The wooden baby was still hungry. There was nothing left to eat in the cottage, so it went out and waddled off down the road to the village. It could not walk very fast because it was so fat. Before long it met a little girl. She was riding along on a new bicycle, ringing the bell and enjoying the swishing sound of the tyres on the warm road.

The baby stopped and the girl ran into it. It was so fat she just bounced off. She picked up her bicycle and glared crossly. She was a very rude little girl, with a curl in the middle of her forehead.

'Hey, Fatty,' she said, 'whatever have you been eating to get a tum like that?'

The wooden baby rolled its eyes and answered:

> *I've eaten, I've gobbled:*
> *Some turnip porridge,*
> *One pail of milk,*
> *One loaf of bread,*
> *A tablecloth,*
> *My mummy, my daddy —*
> *And I'll eat you too!*

And it did. Before the little girl could move the baby sprang on her and gobbled her up, bicycle and all. She put the brakes on as she went down its throat, but that could not save her.

The wooden baby went on its way. Before long it met a farmer bringing a load of hay from a meadow. It stood in the middle of the road, and the horse had to stop.

The farmer leaned down and cracked his whip. 'Out of my way, Puffy Guts!' he shouted.

The wooden baby just blinked at him, licking its lips. Then it began its song again.

> *I've eaten, I've gobbled:*
> *Some turnip porridge,*
> *One pail of milk,*
> *One loaf of bread,*
> *A tablecloth,*
> *My mummy, my daddy,*
> *A girl with a bicycle —*
> *And I'll eat you too!*

The farmer snorted. 'Oh no you won't!' he said. 'It would take more than a fat freak like you to —'

But the baby swallowed him before he could finish the sentence, and the horse and cart as well. All this lot took a bit of eating, but the baby was getting hungrier and hungrier. The strange thing was that the more it ate the greedier it got. To start with, it had not liked things like Mog's bonnet and Krog's boots, but now it was ready for anything. When it had finished the horse it gave a belch like a cannon going off. Then it continued on its way.

Just down the road was a man driving pigs home from market. The wooden baby did not stop to say hello. It simply opened its mouth and sucked them all in.

The baby was now beginning to feel a bit sick. Its tummy rumbled. Its eyes were popping. It could not walk straight. But when it saw a shepherd in a field rounding up his sheep it thought to itself, 'Another little snack won't do any harm.' So it gobbled them up too: the sheep, the shepherd, and even the sheep dog, who was called Mungo and went down the baby's throat wagging his tail and making the horrible creature cough and splutter.

The wooden baby staggered on, its body all swollen and aching with what it had eaten. There really was no room for any more – but the baby was so greedy it could not help wanting more.

'Food!' it chanted. 'Food! Food! Food! *I want food to eat!*'

Its voice was not loud and shattering now, because its stomach was full up. The people and things it had swallowed whole rattled about inside it as it waddled along.

Now, on the outskirts of the village, in a house with a thatched roof and a twisted chimney, lived an old woman called Mother Bunch. Mother Bunch had a face like a potato. She wore a man's cap and was not afraid of anyone or anything. People said she was a witch.

Mother Bunch was out in her garden hoeing cabbages when she saw what looked like a drunken hippopotamus walking down the road. Only it was not a drunken hippopotamus. It was the wooden baby. She leant on her hoe and she began to laugh.

The nearer the creature came the louder she laughed. She slapped her skinny sides and the tears streamed down her face, which was all crisscross-cobwebbed with lines.

The baby stopped. 'What do you think you're laughing at?' it growled, resting its great bulky belly on her gate.

The gate buckled and smashed under the weight of it. Mother Bunch laughed even louder. She pointed at the baby, speechless with glee.

'*What do you think you're laughing at?*' howled the baby, stepping into the garden on its wobbly legs.

Mother Bunch danced in and out of the cabbage patch, round and round the wooden baby. She prodded at it with her hoe. The baby shook with rage. It bent down and tore up a fistful of cabbages. It stuffed the cabbages into its mouth.

'WHAHHAYOUMPHFINKUUMLAUGHMPHINGPHSPLAT?' roared the baby, its mouth full of cabbage.

'You!' shrieked Mother Bunch.

'Me?' said the wooden baby.

'Yes, you, you great big thumping lumpish horror,' said Mother Bunch, giving it another prod with her hoe. 'And you can leave my cabbages alone!'

The baby spat out a half-eaten cabbage. 'What did you call me?' it demanded furiously.

'A monster,' said Mother Bunch.

The baby rolled its eyes. 'Right,' it said.

'Right what?' said Mother Bunch. 'Right what, you silly bushel?'

The baby's face turned purple with fury. Its enormous stomach heaved. In a very quiet and sinister voice it began to sing its song.

I've eaten, I've gobbled:
Some turnip porridge,
One pail of milk,
One loaf of bread,
A tablecloth,
My mummy, my daddy,
A girl with a bicycle,
A farmer with his hay,
A pigman with his pigs,
A shepherd with his sheep,
Cabbages, cabbages —
And I'm going to eat you too!

'That,' said Mother Bunch, 'is what *you* think.' And quick as could be, before the wooden baby had time to jump on her and gobble her up, she pushed her hoe in its belly and cut it open right across.

The wooden baby rolled over on the cabbage patch.

It kicked its legs three times in the air.

Then it stopped kicking.

It was dead.

And then, what a sight there was! Because out of the hole Mother Bunch had cut with her hoe in the wooden baby jumped the sheep dog, Mungo. And after Mungo came the shepherd. And after the shepherd the lambs came leaping. Mungo barked. He rounded up all the sheep, and the shepherd whistled, and they all set off for home.

There was a little pause. And then out of the hole Mother Bunch had cut with her hoe in the wooden baby came the pigs, grunting and squealing, followed by the pigman, wiping his hands on his trousers as though he had been somewhere dirty. They set off home after the shepherd.

And then came the horse and cart, and the farmer with his whip, and the little girl with her brand-new bicycle. And they set off for home after the pigman.

And then, last of all, out jumped the woodcutter and his wife. They were so pleased to be free and alive again that they did a dance of joy, in and out of the cabbages. Mother Bunch shook her head.

'Go home, you silly couple, and be content with what you have,' she said.

Mog curtsied. Krog bowed.

'We will! We will!' they cried together. 'Oh thank you, Mother Bunch! Thank you very much for saving us from the terrible wooden baby!'

'Rubbish,' said Mother Bunch. 'I saved you from yourselves.'

Krog scratched his head. 'I don't understand what you mean,' he said slowly.

'Of course you don't,' snapped Mother Bunch, 'because you haven't got any trousers on!'

Krog looked down. It was true. The wooden baby had not eaten his moleskin trousers and they were still at home. He set off at top speed, his white legs twinkling in the evening sun. And Mog followed after, singing hymns and stopping now and again to think what Mother Bunch could have meant by saying that she had saved them from themselves. But after a while she just sang hymns.

True Thomas

There was once a boy called Thomas. He lived at Ercildoune, a small market town in the country of Berwickshire, in Scotland. His full name was Thomas Learmont, and people say that he was born about 1225. But when he was still young something strange happened to him which made everyone forget his ordinary name and call him True Thomas, or Thomas the Rhymer. This is the story of what that strange thing was.

It started one evening in early summer. Thomas was walking home alone along the banks of a river called the Leader Water. The air was soft and sweet. Butterflies floated on the light like little commas. The hawthorn was in bloom, as white as milk. All down the hillside the breeze was writing sentences in the whin, so that it looked as if the hills were scribbled with gold, crooked golden streams running into the Leader Water, which itself ran green and blue over the chattering pebbles of its bed.

Everywhere Thomas raised his eyes was white and gold, as if the sun in its journeys round the earth had spun a web of light which now glittered between the branches of the trees. His gaze grew dazzled by it, so that he concentrated on the innocent blue of the river instead. He walked along slowly, humming to himself, wondering if he might see a good fat trout in the shadow of the river bank, and catch it in his hands, and take it home to cook for his supper.

He did not see a fish but he saw a queen. Going round a bend in the Leader Water he heard music coming towards him. Thomas looked up. Riding along the bank on a horse the colour of shadows was a beautiful lady. She wore a gown of silk as green as grass. Her hair was long and golden as the whin. Her eyes reminded Thomas of violets he had once seen in a deep wood. Her neck and her forehead were as white as feathers fallen from the wings of a flying swan, but her cheeks shone like red apples.

The music was made by dozens of tiny crystal bells that gossiped on the mane of the lady's horse. The horse's bridle made a separate sound, very clear and frosty. Together the two tunes were perfect, and it seemed as though the air itself turned into music as the lady smiled.

Thomas snatched off this cap and knelt before her. She was so bonny he was sure she must be the Queen of Heaven. 'Hail, Mary!' he cried. 'Hail, Queen of Heaven!'

The lady shook her head gently. She dismounted from her horse. 'No, Thomas,' she said. 'I am not the Queen of Heaven. I am the Queen of Elphame.'

Thomas was frightened when he heard this. If she was not a good spirit, he thought, then she must be a bad spirit. And if she was not the Queen of Heaven then perhaps she was the Queen of Hell. As for Elphame – he had never heard of it.

'What do you want with me?' he asked boldly, though he did not feel bold.

'I want your voice,' said the Queen of Elphame. 'But first you must give me seven years of your life.'

'My voice?' said Thomas. 'How can you have that? And how can I give you seven years?'

The Queen of Elphame did not answer him. Instead she held up her right hand and waved it in the evening air. Immediately there were blue birds going round and round her wrist in a circle, a bright bracelet of birds, lovely to look at. Then she held up her left hand and waved that also. On the instant there were green birds going round and round that wrist, another bracelet, winging in the opposite direction. Thomas could not take his eyes off the two circles, the one blue, the one green, the little flickering wings, the swift bird-bracelets.

He began to feel drowsy. His head was full of the sweetness of the hawthorn blossom. Tears came to his eyes.

'Now it is time to go,' said the Queen of Elphame.

She kissed the neck of the horse the colour of shadows, then she mounted it. Thomas climbed up behind her. They rode off together. Blue and green birds, shaken free from the Queen of Elphame's wrists, whirled around their heads as the horse rode over the Leader Water. Thomas thought he must be dreaming.

All he could see was the white of the Queen of Elphame's neck and the gold of her streaming hair. All he could hear was the crystal music of the little bells. The horse galloped fast. The horse galloped faster. Then the horse was galloping and galloping so fast that the trees and the river, the hills and the sky became one blur, and then not even a blur.

The music of the bells was like an alphabet in another language. Green and gold, white and blue, Thomas's world spun about his head and burst in his eyes. Green, sang the bells. And white, sang the bells. And blue, sang the bells. And gold gold gold, sang the bells. These colours were all that Thomas could think.

Then the colours went out and the horse slowed down and the song of the bells grew softer and Thomas saw that they had reached the edge of a desert. Thomas had never seen a desert before, but something told him that even if he travelled the whole world over he would never again see one like this. This desert seemed to begin at the end of all he had ever known. It was perfectly flat and empty. There were no colours anywhere.

It was a place where you would meet no one because there was no one to meet. It was a place where you would lose your shadow if you walked there for long. It was a place where if you wrote your name in the sand it would soon disappear for ever, leaving not even a dot behind. North, south, east and west, as far as the eye could see, this terrible desert stretched. The Queen of Elphame drew rein and the horse stopped.

'Thomas,' she said, 'do you see the road that we must take?'

Thomas stared at the desert.

'No,' he said. 'I can see nothing. Only desert.'

'Look more closely,' said the Queen of Elphame.

Thomas rubbed his eyes. He stared at the desert, trying to make sense of it. It was then that he saw three roads. The first road ran towards the north from where they stood. It was narrow and twisty and as Thomas looked along it the way seemed dark with thorns and briars.

'What road is that?' he asked the Queen of Elphame.

'That is the road to Heaven,' she answered. 'It is a hard road, as you see. We shall not take it.'

Thomas looked at the second road. The second road ran towards the south

"The Queen of Elphame drew rein and the horse stopped."

from where they stood. It was wide and straight and seemed to run downhill all the way through fields of lilies.

'What road is that?' asked Thomas.

'That is the road to Hell,' said the Queen of Elphame. 'It is an easy road, as you see. We shall not take it.'

Thomas looked at the third road. The third road ran towards the west from where they stood. It was narrow in some places and wide in others. There were flowers here and there beside it, but also nettles. It went up hill and down dale, and sometimes it was straight and sometimes twisty.

'What road is that?' asked Thomas.

'That is the road to Elphame,' said the Queen. 'It is a hard road and an easy road, as you see. Only those who can stand still in themselves can go down it. Only those who know that they know nothing can find the way. Others may point it out, but no one can walk it for anyone else. It is not the road of yes or no, but the road of road. And you and I must take it.'

The horse the colour of shadow moved forward. Thomas and the Queen of Elphame started down the third road. On and on they went. It grew dark and then darker. There was no moon in the sky above them, and no stars shone.

Once Thomas thought he could hear the sound of something like the sea, but it was a curious inside-out kind of sound, so that instead of waves breaking on rocks it sounded more like rocks breaking on waves. After that he heard nothing: no birds, no words, no wind, no echoes; nothing. The horse's hooves made no noise at all on the road and the bells on its mane did not ring any more. Everywhere was black and silence.

At long last Thomas saw a tiny speck of light in front of them. They rode on and the speck of light grew bigger and brighter. Now it was as big as a fist, now it was as big as a man's head, now it was as big as a whole man, then it burst about them like a wave, a bright foam of light, towering and splashing, and Thomas saw that they had come out of the dark into a fine country. There were green trees and green rivers, blue hills as fat as pumpkins, valleys full of feathery blue-green grass, white fountains, gold mountains, and green birds and blue birds everywhere. The crystal bells rang on the mane of the horse the colour of shadows, and its bridle chimed, and there were bells on every branch keeping time with that tossing music, and more bells bouncing on the crests of the fountains, and bells on the birds as they flew. Everything seemed to rhyme with everything else. Everywhere was light and music.

The Queen of Elphame drew rein and the horse stopped. They dismounted in a walled garden. In the garden was a maze. They walked round and round in the maze until they came to the middle. A gold tree grew there. There was one silver apple on the tree. The Queen of Elphame plucked the silver apple and handed it to Thomas.

'Eat this,' she said. 'Eat this, and Thomas of Ercildoune will be True Thomas.'

Thomas took a bite from the silver apple. 'True Thomas!' he said. 'What do you mean?'

The Queen of Elphame smiled and did not answer. Thomas ate the rest of the silver apple. It tasted of night and white and gold and music. It tasted of desert and bells and hawthorn blossoms. It tasted of birds in a circle and all that had ever been, and was, and would be. It was an apple that gave Thomas the twisty power to speak straight in rhyme of what had not yet happened, and the hard power to foretell future events as easily as if he had already seen them pass. It was because of the powers of the silver apple that he could be known as True Thomas. The name of the apple was Truth.

When even the pips were gone the Queen of Elphame took Thomas to her glass castle. It was a shining place. The fires that burned in the grates were made of diamonds. Bright harps hung in the air and played when the Queen looked at them. The floor was paved with sunlight and instead of doors there were rainbows. Peacocks strutted up and down on the lawns outside, talking in Latin and Greek. Strange plants grew in the Queen's garden, with labels round their necks to tell you what they were called: triolets, odes, epodes, sestinas, cantos, centos, and sonnets.

The Queen's servants brought Thomas a cloak of grass-green silk and shoes of moss-green velvet. He lived in Elphame for seven years. The bells rang, the fountains sang, the hills stood blue and still with birds above them, and Thomas walked and talked with the Queen each day from morning to evening. She told him all sorts of secrets and instructed him in all manner of mysteries. She taught him that everything is related to everything, and that a poet is only a man like other men but more so, having the power to see likeness where others see opposites. She taught him to bind things up in words to follow the lines that linked them, to make a net like the stars in the sky, wide-meshed but letting nothing slip through. She taught him how to think in images and how to feel in words. She taught him that man is a fragment who can be whole. She taught him that there are things which words alone can talk about, and other things which all the words in the world cannot say. The seven years passed quickly. To Thomas they seemed no longer than seven days.

At last his time was up. Thomas had to return across the blackness and the silence, along the third road through the desert, on and on until he got back to Scotland. Settled once more in the little town of Ercildoune, he never forgot his meeting with the Queen of Elphame, his journey to her strange and beautiful country, and all that he had learned there when he ate the silver apple. He wrote poems and songs, and went up and down in Scotland telling or singing them to all who would listen.

Some of his poems spoke of things that had not yet happened but which did happen while he was still living among men. Some of them told of things which did not happen for centuries to come, but when the time came they also came true. There are still some left yet to come true.

When Thomas was an old man the Queen of Elphame came once more for him. Just as she had done before, she rode in early summer along the banks of the Leader Water on her horse the colour of shadows, the small bells making music as she came.

'Thomas,' she cried, 'True Thomas, my Thomas, your time has come. Not for seven years, but now for evermore you shall be mine.'

Then Thomas mounted the horse the colour of shadows behind the Queen of Elphame and rode away with her. He lives in her perfect country on the far side of the desert and the silence, along the long third road that is both twisty and straight, and hard and easy, where there are green trees and green rivers, blue hills as fat as pumpkins, valleys full of feathery blue-green grass, white fountains, gold mountains, and green birds and blue birds, birds everywhere; and he lives for evermore.

Some notes on the stories

I remember James Reeves once advising me not to reveal the sources for my stories. To do so, according to that fine and now neglected poet and storyteller, was a bit like publishing recipes for dishes after the food has been eaten. Any cook knows that the secret is in the cooking. This said, I will still mention some of the ingredients that went to the making of these tales.

HUNG-WU AND THE WITCH'S DAUGHTER comes from China. It has been pointed out that there is nothing of the grand manner about the telling of Chinese folk-stories, while they are often fantastic and deal largely in magic. The best collection of them in English is probably *Strange Stories from a Chinese Studio* (2 vols, 1880) by H. A. Giles, but to be honest I can't remember if I found the bones for my tale there.

LORD FOX is an old English story, a version of the Bluebeard legend first given shape in France by Charles Perrault as *La Barbe-bleue* in his *Histoires et contes du temps passé avec des moralités* (1697). The notion of the husband or dark suitor with the secret chamber full of horrors is more ancient than that. I like to think that Shakespeare heard about it in his childhood in Stratford. In his *Much Ado About Nothing*, Benedick (Act I, Scene 1) alludes to 'the old tale . . . it is not so, nor 'twas not so, but indeed, God forbid it should be so.' And in Edmund Spenser's *The Faerie Queene* (Book III, xi. 54), Britomart comes to a house in which *Be bold, be bold* is written over every door until she comes to the one with *Be not too bold* upon it.

THE WHITE RAVEN is a story I was first told late at night by a Welsh fireside, though in this case I have set my version in 'a far-away country'. The idea of the harper singing for his keep at the great feast, as well as the drowned valley, might tell the reader that this country could be Wales.

THE WITCHES WHO STOLE EYES comes from the country which was called Bohemia before it became Czechoslovakia. These Slavonic stories often feature superhuman dwellers in the woods. The witches in the original are called the Jezinkas.

THE DRAGON KINGDOM dates from tenth-century Japan in its first written version. It is the tale behind the Crane and Turtle dance which was performed as a rite of the Shinto religion on some Japanese holidays (once holy days).

THE KING OF THE BLACK ART is one of those stories which crops up in slightly different versions all over Europe. The Brothers Grimm recorded it in German as *The Magician and his Pupil*, and Norwegian, Russian, Spanish, French, Greek, Scottish and Irish versions are also to be found. The English folk-song 'The Coal-Black Smith' relates to it.

LEFT EYE, RIGHT EYE is another story I picked up in Wales. Notice that it takes the thought of supernatural beings living in wild places so seriously that it does not name them as 'fairies'. There is something in the Welsh carefully calling these pygmy people the 'Fair Family' or 'Lordly Ones' which sends a shiver down the spine. The woman who told me the tale would in fact only utter their name in Welsh. As I recall it, though I am no Welsh scholar and may have the spelling wrong, she called them the Telwyth Teg.

ORPHEUS AND EURYDICE comes straight out of ancient Greek mythology.

THE WOODEN BABY must be another old Bohemian tale, I think. I say this because recently I came across a poem by the Czech poet Miroslav Holub in which he refers to 'the wood-block baby that gobbles up everything', as though this was a creature from a story he had heard in his childhood. All the same, I first heard the story in my childhood, too – from my grandmother, who had certainly not been to Bohemia.

TRUE THOMAS is based on the anonymous fifteenth-century Scottish ballad, 'Thomas the Rimer'. There is a good text of it, with some illuminating notes, in Robert Graves's *English and Scottish Ballads* (1957).